LOBO AND HAWK

One was a Yankee. One was a Rebel. They were the only two survivors of the bombardment of a New Mexico town at the end of the Civil War. After trying unsuccessfully to kill each other, they decided to become partners and go after some Confederate gold that was up for grabs. The trouble was that they weren't the only ones who knew about the hoard. Soon there would be trouble enough to bring back old hostilities, and only blazing guns would settle the matter. But who would live?

Books by Jake Douglas
in the Linford Western Library:

LAREDO'S LAND
RIO GRINGO
RIO REPRISAL
QUICK ON THE TRIGGER
A CORNER OF BOOT HILL
POINT OF NO RETURN
SUNDOWN
SIERRA HIGH
JUDAS PASS

JAKE DOUGLAS

LOBO AND HAWK

Complete and Unabridged

LINFORD
Leicester

First published in Great Britain in 2004 by
Robert Hale Limited
London

First Linford Edition
published 2005
by arrangement with
Robert Hale Limited
London

British Library CIP Data

Douglas, Jake
  Lobo and Hawk.—Large print ed.—
  Linford western library
  1. Western stories
  2. Large type books
  I. Title
  823.9′14 [F]

  ISBN 1–84395–841–4

Published by
F. A. Thorpe (Publishing)
Anstey, Leicestershire

Set by Words & Graphics Ltd.
Anstey, Leicestershire
Printed and bound in Great Britain by
T. J. International Ltd., Padstow, Cornwall

Prologue

March, 1865

The bombardment of Kettledrum, New Mexico, close to the line of what was then Indian Territory, went on for two days without let-up. Artillery of Yankees and Rebs both threw in everything they had, despite the fact that they knew troops under their own flags were somewhere in there.

It was one of many foul-ups towards the end of the Civil War. Union forces found themselves way south of where they figured they should be and a scouting patrol walked in on ragtag Confederate soldiers having their way with Kettledrum and its inhabitants. Word was that the folk here had helped the Yankees on more than one occasion and the Rebs, without any leader above the rank of sergeant, figured it was their

1

bounden duty to show their displeasure at such treacherous behaviour.

They needed ammunition, food, horses — hell, they needed just about everything, including medical attention for their wounded and they set about taking it. Even so, the two doctors in Kettledrum willingly tended the wounded and the folk of the town gave them some of their own meagre supply of food. But there was little ammunition available. However, there was hard drink and the war-weary Rebs took to it like ducks to a pond.

Most of them were drunk, or well on the way to being so, when the Yankee patrol ventured in and a hurried ambush was arranged. But the raw redeye had its effect and the Rebs botched it. It turned into a pitched gun battle, the Yankees apparently having ample supplies of ammunition. They dug in at first and then began a house-to-house hunt for the enemy. The Reb sergeant was the worse for drink and took a shot through the head which left the rest of the Southerners without leadership. One soldier, a big back-woods boy from Tennessee, said,

'Waal, ah dunno about you boys, but ah've about had me a bellyful-an'-a-half of all this shootin' and killin'. It ain't so far to the Big Smokies an' ah aim to take off. Anyone wants to come, ah can guarantee a mighty good feed of pig's liver an' wild onions an' some of the best corn likker you ever will run up against. Ah'm lightin' a shuck an' ah says 'farewell' to them that's stayin' an' 'Let's move' to them that's a'comin' . . . '

About half the Rebs went with him — the only reason the others stayed was because they were in other buildings and didn't know about the mass desertion . . .

Along the way, the deserters ran into a battered batallion of Southerners in full retreat and, quick to cover them-selves, they told the captain that Yankees had taken over the town. During the confusion while artillery was set up and ranging shots were taken, the deserters slipped away — and the first of hundreds of rounds of explosive shells fell on Kettledrum.

On the far side of the town, on the slopes of Curlew Hill, the captain of the Yankee soldiers who had sent the patrol into Kettledrum to scout the ground, immediately set up his artillery and began answering the rebel forces. Many rounds fell short and Kettledrum was subsequently systematically converted to rubble.

Clapboard structures and frame houses exploded into flaming match-wood. The few brick buildings were reduced to rubble and red dust. The streets were blasted into a series of overlapping holes and bodies were flung through the air, blown to pieces, regardless of what uniform they wore — or if they wore no uniform at all — civilian clothes, either dresses or trousers, were no protection against the rain of death that tore the Southern skies apart and churned the landscape into a bloodstained heap of rubble until first the Rebel forces and soon after the Union ones ran low on ammunition.

The Confederate captain swept the smoking ruins briefly with his field glasses, grunted to his lieutenant that no one could live through that, and then gave the order to continue the retreat.

On Curlew Hill, the Union captain watched the ragged Southern forces abandon their now useless cannon and called for pursuit. They skirted the slaughterhouse of Kettledrum, riding hard after the fleeing Rebs, convinced their patrol had been utterly destroyed in the early stages of the bombardment.

'No man could survive that hell,' commented the Yankee captain and his second-in-command agreed, adding,

'Sure glad I didn't pull the short straw for leading that patrol in there.'

The captain glared. 'Take ten men and cut across country to the river. You ride hard, you'll beat the Rebs there.

Set up an ambush — and I don't expect to find a single Reb alive when I get there . . . '

The officer flushed, swallowed and saluted, wheeling his weary mount to carry out his orders.

★ ★ ★

But both the Yankee and the Rebel commanders were wrong.

There were two men who had survived that thundering rain from hell that had smashed an entire town flat into the countryside.

One Union sergeant.

One Confederate private.

They were both extremely low on ammunition but that didn't stop them from doing their best to kill each other when they met in the smoking ruins amongst the shattered corpses just before sundown of that bloody day.

When the bullets ran out they would have their bayonets — or their clasp knives, or a length of shattered timber, a rock — *their bare hands!*

Each was determined that the other would die with all the rest that had gone to meet their Maker this day.

1

Alamosa — 1868

Myron Hatfield wasn't looking for trouble when he dropped off the nine-car freight just outside of Alamosa in the San Luis Valley of Colorado that spring day in '68.

He had no saddle with him, only a sagging warbag and a battered Colt Dragoon pistol rammed into the length of plaited rawhide he was using to hold up his worn and dirt-stiff trousers. His boots were run-over at the heels — designed more for riding than walking — but he had walked more miles than he cared to count these last few years. His shirt was patched, sweat-stained, collar and cuffs frayed. No vest. His hat was curled and ragged at the brim.

He was unshaven, begrimed, ragged

thick brown hair covering his neck. He knew he looked exactly what he was — a drifter and he was *hungry*. Man, he could eat a horse and use the shoe nails to pick his teeth — which weren't in great shape, either.

So he approached the bustling town warily, using what features of the landscape he could on his approach into town.

But he was too eager, his belly rumbling against his backbone, and the waiting sheriff stepped out from behind a leg of the water tower and lifted a big, broken-knuckled hand.

He was a large man, not too unfriendly of face, but he had a jaw that stretched from here to the sierras and back, looking like a piece of them that had broken off. No give in this lawman, Hatfield decided, and swore softly.

'Depot's half a mile down the track, mister. Now what for would a wolf-lean *hombre* like you want to drop off early and walk in? I'd say your boots don't need the exercise. And nor do you.'

Hatfield sighed and lifted his hands out from his sides to show he wasn't on the prod. The sheriff's hands hung loosely at his sides now, but the right one was close in against his holstered Colt.

'All right, Sheriff. I'm caught — I rode the rails in. But all I want is some grub and if I can't find work I'll be on my way.'

'You'll be on your way as soon as I say you will. You got a name?'

Hatfield told him, volunteering nothing more. He had learnt a long time back never to give more information than was required for an answer.

'From up north, I'd say.'

'Originally the Dakotas.'

The sheriff waited for more and when nothing was forthcoming asked, 'Why didn't you go back after the War?'

'Nothin' to go back for.'

'So you stayed on here, hopin' to make your fortune outta us poor white trash that you beat down but never properly whipped.'

Hatfield smiled wryly, spreading his arms. 'It must've slipped right through my fingers, then.'

The lawman studied him with hard eyes, mildly surprised that Hatfield held his gaze with blue eyes that had a kind of chill to them. 'How much money you got?'

'Enough for a little grub, dependin' on prices.'

'Not enough to keep you in my town — you need at least enough for three days' stay. Man can't find work in that time, I don't want him here anyway.'

'I aim to look for work.'

The sheriff shook his head slowly. 'No — there's another town fifty miles down track. I'm willin' to turn my back while you jump back on one of them freight cars when the train pulls out.'

Hatfield felt his empty belly tighten. *This was one hard son of a bitch!*

'Lemme grab some food first, Sheriff. I'll clear town then if you want.'

'Told you what you'd do. Now this train'll be here in a couple of hours. Till then you and me're gonna sit in the shade here and when you hear that whistle blow, you climb aboard and I'll wave you off — like this.'

The sheriff lifted his left hand in a brief wave and Hatfield's gaze instinctively swept towards it. Immediately he knew he shouldn't have fallen for it as he heard the Colt slide from leather and he swung back, lifting his left arm to ward off the blow. The gun barrel cracked hard against his bony forearm and he grunted in pain, struck out instinctively, his right fist cracking against the lawman's jaw.

The sheriff was obviously surprised as he reeled back. He was even more surprised when Hatfield stepped in and sank a fist into his hard belly, hooked with an elbow to the side of his head, and kicked his legs from under him.

As the lawman sprawled, Hatfield turned to run: there was only the open country — no use going into the town. That was the sheriff's stamping ground and he likely knew it as well as he knew his own name. So Hatfield stumbled across the gleaming railroad tracks and almost made it into a line of chaparral when the first bullet kicked gravel against his legs and the second made a hornet snarl alongside his left ear.

He stopped, lifting his hands shoulder-high without turning around.

He heard the sheriff's heavy tread crunching across the blue metal and then a gun barrel crashed behind his right ear and he fell to his knees, the world spinning. A boot took him between the shoulders and shoved him face-down against a railroad tie, splinters tearing at his stubbled face.

'Try to play square with you drifters, but you ain't forgot the goddamn War, have you? Think us Southern boys are a bunch of hicks with all our brains in the seat of our pants — well, you gonna get a taste of our famous Southern hospitality, Yankee. First in my cell, then on my chain gang. You gonna be lucky to walk outta here this side of Christmas. How you like that . . . ?'

To punctuate the question, the sheriff drove a boot against Hatfield's ribs, rolling the man half on to his back.

'Now get up and walk ahead of me or I'll blow you out from under that hat!'

* * *

Deputy Chris Winters figured that, with a little luck, he could wind up this manhunt by sundown.

Magraw had been way ahead of him but the latest sign showed his horse was laming, likely a piece of sharp gravel from the sierra trail under a shoe. There weren't too many places the fugitive could go up here and Winters figured he would make for the obvious place — a ledge that overlooked the trail and would give him a good sweep with the rifle. He knew the man was using an old Spencer, still a deadly weapon in its heavy .52 calibre, but the rimfire ammunition was old now and lacked punch. Chris was armed with a Henry repeater in .44 rimfire and he knew a trail that would put him above the ledge and give him a good target area.

He moved his black horse off the regular trail when he came to a narrow-looking draw which caused most folk to ride on by without bothering to explore it. But the draw opened out after a hundred yards and there was an easy rise to the slopes above through timber and brush.

The black knew this area for Chris had once tracked a red deer in here that had been wounded by a drunken cowhand just looking for something to shoot at. To this day that cowhand would have a reminder of the incident in the splayed and crookedly frozen fingers of his right hand where Chris's boot heel had ground into it after he had despatched the gut-shot animal.

Now he was chasing down a man who had just as little regard for any kind of life — Magraw, a Texan who figured the world should step aside when it saw him coming, and he was ready and willing to shoot it down if it didn't. He had had a long run and there was a string of wanted dodgers out on him across the southwest. Magraw had made the mistake of coming to Alamosa and letting his short fuse get the better of him. He had shot and killed a barman in the Century saloon, wounded a dancehall girl on the way out and stolen Warren Halliday's bay gelding which he had changed for a racy sorrel he had waiting in a draw.

'This son of a bitch has dodgers on him from the Rio to the Rockies,' Sheriff Atwater had growled while Chris packed his gear for the manhunt. 'Three of 'em are for 'dead or alive'. So bring him in dead and the world's gonna be a leetle bit better for it.'

Good enough for Chris Winters. He'd heard about Magraw before and his wild ways, leaving maimed and broken women behind him and the occasional dead man. It would be a pleasure to nail the bastard.

The trail out to the slope above the ledge lost its cover quickly for a man on horseback, so Chris ground-hitched the black back amongst the trees, took his rifle and spare ammunition, field glasses and his canteen and made his way through sun-baked boulders. It was a hot day now, the open slopes blasting the heat down across that ledge below. He settled amongst some sandstone rocks and used the glasses to locate Magraw. Just as he had figured — the man was sprawled amongst some low rocks where he could command a view of the trail he expected to see the deputy using. His horse was back amongst bigger boulders, favouring the right foreleg, holding the hoof above the ground, confirming Chris's belief there was a stone under the shoe. The man hadn't even taken time to prise the stone out and give the animal some relief.

The deputy settled in, took a swig of water, levered a shell into the Henry's breech and sighted down to the ledge. He couldn't get a good shot at Magraw, but he saw the canteen lying on the ground — in the sun, too, which was typical of the man's slovenly habits.

Chris squeezed off two fast shots and the canteen jerked and skidded away, blasted open, water spraying. A third shot sent the smashed vessel over the ledge and now Magraw was going to be a mighty thirsty man before long . . .

Magraw himself rolled quickly when the canteen exploded beside him, splashing him with warm water, and as the echoes of the shots slapped away across the slope, Winters thought he heard him curse. Magraw twisted on to his back and got off one booming shot with the Spencer, the heavy slug tearing a track in the loose scree of the slope off to the deputy's left.

'Not even close, Magraw,' Chris called down and put another slug from the Henry into the space between the rocks where the outlaw sprawled. This time he heard the man's curse plainly. 'How you want it to be, Magraw? Shoot it out or throw down your gun now and I take you back to town?'

'Where that goddamn Atwater's just waitin' to slip a noose around my neck? Like hell!'

Magraw flopped on to his back and the big Spencer thundered again, this time the bullet chewing splinters of rock only a foot from the deputy's shoulder. The man was a good shot now he had pinpointed Winters and Chris slithered back, moved away a few yards, snapped a shot, then rolled back to his original position.

Magraw put a bullet into the place where Chris had taken his pot-shot and he raised himself over the rocks to do so. Chris shot him through the left shoulder and the man sprawled over the rocks with an involuntary scream of pain. He lost the Spencer, the short-barrelled carbine spilling from his grip and sliding part way down the slope.

The lawman had levered in another shell already and he shot the killer in the right leg as he flailed around there. Magraw yelled curses at him, voice echoing through the hills.

'Animals feel pain, too, Magraw! Specially gut-shot ones. Want me to let you find out what it's like?'

'Goddamn you, Winters! What you gonna do? Shoot me to pieces, you murderin' son of a bitch!'

'That's rich, coming from you. Yeah, I could shoot you apart a little at a time, and it wouldn't bother me, but it's hot out here and I want to get back to town. So, I'll give you your choice once again — toss out your pistol and crawl out where I can see you in full, or stay put and die.'

More curses and then a battered Gunnison and Griswald revolver skidded across the dust and Magraw raised his hands, his left one only a few inches because of the pain in his shoulder.

'Crawl out of the rocks,' ordered the deputy and the outlaw swore again, crawled and floundered awkwardly away from the rocks.

When he was about ten feet clear, Chris called that that was far enough, stood up and started to make his way down the slope, Henry held at the ready. He was almost to the bottom when his boots skidded a little and he stumbled.

Bloody and filthy, Magraw's right hand lifted from his side and there was a small Navy Colt in it, swinging towards Winters. As it cracked in a single shot, Chris heaved himself to the side and, still in mid-air, twisted and fired the long-barrelled Henry. He hit rolling, levering as he came out of the roll and lifted to one knee. His shot had sprayed gravel into Magraw's face and the man clawed at his eyes, then started firing the Navy Colt blindly.

One shot burned across Chris's upper left arm and then he beaded quickly and blew Magraw to hell with a bullet through the middle of his snarling face.

The deputy fumbled to get a neckerchief tied about his slight wound and glanced up at the sky.

Nice timing: the sun would be down in about fifteen minutes, giving him just enough time to load Magraw's body on to the bay gelding after he prised the stone out from under its shoe, and get down out of the sierras before dark.

He could make the ride back to Alamosa by midnight, he figured.

*   *   *

He did, and Sheriff Atwater was pleased that Magraw had been killed, offered his deputy a shot of redeye and told him to go get the arm wound attended to by Doc Julius.

'Then grab a little supper and get back here — you got the night-duty this week, don't forget.'

'Thanks, Sheriff — I really 'preciate that after two days in the sierras and a gunfight!'

Atwater merely glared. 'You draw night-duty, you do it.'

'S'pose I hadn't got in till sunup?'

'Then you'd have an extra night to make up, wouldn't you?'

'You're all heart, Sheriff.'

23

'And you're wastin' time.'

The sheriff was still at the law office when Chris got back from the doctor's. Atwater reached for his hat and started towards the street door.

'Only one prisoner. Some smart-mouth Yankee drifter,' Atwater said on the way out. 'Made him wait for his supper but you can give him breakfast on time.'

The sheriff closed the door behind him and Chris swore softly, hung up his hat, running fingers through his long yellow hair. He rolled a cigarette, flexing his left arm which was stiffening a little, then, just as he was sitting down he figured he'd check on the prisoner first.

He took a lamp from the desk and went down the passage. Atwater had put the man in the last cell in the block. It was the draughtiest and leaked when it rained. But then the sheriff hated everything Yankee with a passion. Some said it was because a Yankee ball had removed one of his testicles at the

Battle of The Wilderness, but Atwater wasn't the kind of man you asked to confirm or deny such rumours.

The man was dozing on his bunk but he stirred when light from the lamp washed across his battered, beard-shagged face. Which reminded Chris that he wanted a shave badly, but it would have to wait till morning as his gear was back in his room.

'You OK in there, feller?' the deputy asked as Myron Hatfield stirred, holding a hand to shade his eyes.

'You ain't Atwater.'

'Deputy Chris Winters — got the night-duty.'

'Oh, yeah — heard part of it earlier. Passage acts like a soundin' board.' He swung his legs off the bunk and came across. Winters saw the dried blood on his neck where it had trickled down from behind his ear. It was typical of Atwater that he hadn't allowed Hatfield to clean up before throwing him in the cell.

'See you resisted arrest.'

Hatfield touched the bloody ear with a rueful smile. 'Made a mistake — he slugged me and I slugged back. Oughta know by now not to take a poke at these hick lawman — *hey*!'

Suddenly he leaned closer, squinting a little, moving his head so the bars didn't throw any part of Winters' face into shadow.

'What?' asked the deputy, leerily, frowning.

'*Hawk*! By God, it *is* you!'

The deputy stiffened, looking sharply at the prisoner.

'Name's Chris Winters, feller. You've got the wrong man.'

'The hell I have! Oh, sure, your name might be Chris Winters, same as mine's Myron Hatfield — but when we met a few years ago in what was left of a town called Kettledrum, I called myself 'Lobo' and you said to call you 'Hawk'! Now don't tell me you don't recollect *that*!'

2

Back to Kettledrum

Hell, he could never forget that day in March 1865 when the whole damn town was wiped off the map . . .

He was choking on dust, a thick phlegm forming in the back of his throat, giving rise to a slight panic when he couldn't draw in air nor cough it out. One hard effort finally removed the plug and he spat, air wheezing and gurgling down his throat as he sat up slowly, still partly dazed, thick layers of dust and a few pieces of splintered wood and broken brick falling from the uniform jacket.

Instinctively, he groped for his rifle, a prized Spencer carbine taken from a dead Yankee on the banks of Murdering Creek. He had also taken a square leather box containing spare magazines, but during the fight with the Union patrol in Kettledrum here he knew he had used up much of the ammunition. In fact, he was pretty sure he remembered slapping home the last magazine through the butt. How many shots had he fired since . . . ? Must be close to the limit — seven . . .

His ears were ringing with the aftermath of the long bombardment and he felt disoriented, staggering when he stood, groping for something to hold on to. There was nothing even half his height left standing in the rubble where he was and the Spencer was too short to use as a support. He stood as still as he could until the dizziness passed and clawed dust from his eyes, looking around at the devastation.

Christ! How had he lived through those two days of hell? More importantly — had anyone else survived . . . ?

He stumbled away from the rubble, found Carson and Willard — or what was left of them — and tumbled down some debris to partially cover them.

What else could he do . . . ? Anyway, what did it matter? If you were dead, nothing mattered.

He almost fell, spinning around as he heard a sound behind him — a slithering of rubble, but somehow it didn't have a natural sound. There was movement, a dark shape rearing up on the far side of what had been a wall, where some of the Yankees had been dug-in. A hand moved and there was a crack and a spurt of flame-tinged smoke and he heard the thrum of a bullet past his ear.

The Johnny Reb dropped to one knee, the old training taking over, and the Spencer rose to his shoulder and he fired. Just the one shot — he was actually surprised that there had been a live round still left in the tin magazine. Dust flew from the Yankee's shoulder and the man staggered. But he was game and he got off another shot before flinging himself behind a crumbling section of wall.

The Reb jumped up and ran after

him, Spencer hammer cocked, but he was pretty sure there wasn't a round in the breech. The lever hadn't felt as if it had met much resistance when he had worked it, which likely meant the magazine was empty. *His pistol*. Hell, he was still groggy, not thinking clearly.

There was a Remington Army .44 rammed into his belt under the torn grey jacket and he groped for it, checked the cylinder. Three loads. That ought to be enough — unless the Yankee led him into a trap where some of his friends were waiting . . .

They stalked each other for most of what remained of the day, exchanging only a few shots each. In fact, the Southerner was mad at himself for firing the last shot in the Remington. The Yankee had ambushed him nicely and it was only pure luck that his ball had missed. It had slapped through the broad, ragged brim of the Reb's hat, burned the tip of one ear as he ducked, spun and triggered before he could stop himself. He knew he had missed and the waste of his last bullet made him madder still.

The Yankee had fired once more and then he heard him running off down what had been a side street, somewhere between the old bank building and a drug store if he recollected correctly. The Reb had gone after him, determined to finish the man. By now they were both convinced that they were the only two left alive in Kettledrum.

Two men — enemies — each representing his beliefs and cause. They had to try to kill each other: there was no other way. Even if they were both sick to their bellies with killing and seeing their friends maimed or blown apart, trying to identify mangled piles of meat that were found where they recalled having seen comrades earlier — but the War wasn't yet over and it was their duty to kill every man not wearing the right uniform.

It was late in the afternoon, down by the creek, when the Reb staggered out of some brush and surprised the Yankee washing the wound in his shoulder. The Northerner snatched up his pistol, falling backwards as he fired. The shot went into the trees and when he pulled the trigger again the hammer fell on an empty chamber. The sun's glow was ruddy but suddenly the Yankee's begrimed face looked very white.

The Reb swung the Spencer into line, hammer cocking, and the Yankee watched with wide eyes, lifting his hands out from his sides, letting the Colt drop into the shallows.

'You win, Reb,' he croaked and he sounded mighty weary, almost relieved.

'On your feet!'

It took a lot for the Yankee to clamber upright and he swayed, watery blood trickling down his left arm. Then the Johnny Reb swore just as his finger tightened on the carbine's trigger.

'Hell with it. I've had me a gutful of killing!' He jerked the Spencer's barrel. 'Go on. Git!'

The Northerner stared at him, uncomprehending.

'You don't move in about two seconds, friend, I'll blow you to glory! I'm giving you a chance and you'd better take it!'

The Yankee swallowed, licked his lips, stared and nodded once. Then, holding the slight wound in his shoulder, he turned and plunged across the shallow creek, disappearing into the brush. The Reb stood there, listening to the man move away from him and he grinned tightly as he tossed the empty, useless rifle aside.

That Yank would never know he was running from a man without a single bullet within reach!

★　★　★

It rained and turned cold that night, and the Reb made himself a rough shelter that kept him mostly dry, but he would have given anything for a packet of vestas and a fire. He was used to discomfort after four years in the Confederate army and huddled in a corner of his lean-to with collar turned up and hat brim pulled down. Still, water trickled between his collar and his neck and soaked his trousers, and he was almost at the point of dozing off when he smelled smoke.

The Yankee! Son of a gun must have a fire going! Well, the man still wouldn't know that the Southerner's Spencer was empty and if he could get close to some flames and stop this shivering and —

Hell, what was he hesitating for? The man was the enemy! Go in with knife or broken brick and beat his brains out — take the damn fire!

He started out at once, standing up on a broken horse trough, looking around the flattened town. It was easy to pick out the fire and he figured it was in that same side street between the wreckage of the bank and the druggist's where the Yank had run down earlier. OK. Let's go get some warmth and — man! He could smell food!

That was it. The Yankee was as good

as dead if he had grub as well as fire.

But it didn't quite work out that way.

He walked into a trap. The Yankee was waiting for him amongst the shattered benches and counters and cupboards of the bank. While the Reb stalked the fire, looking for the Yank, salivating at the smell of cooking meat, the Yankee came out behind him and clobbered him with an axe handle. Maybe his hands were wet and slipped on the hickory because the blow didn't land squarely. It knocked off the Reb's hat and dropped him to one knee, but he was far from being out.

He lifted an arm to ward off the second blow, scooped up a handful of mud and hurled it into the Yankee's face. The man gulped and spat as he stumbled back and then the Southerner was upon him, wrenching the axe handle from his grip, slamming it low down across the backs of the man's legs.

The Yankee howled and collapsed and the Johnny Reb stood over him, the handle raised for the killing blow. He hesitated — he had meant it when he had said he'd had a bellyful of killing and this Yankee looked pretty damn helpless, sprawled in the mud, with the flickering light of the fire reaching him from under the crude shelter the man had built out of splintered clapboards.

The Southerner tossed the axe handle into the darkness, reached down and offered a hand to the astonished Northerner. Warily, he took it and the tall man from the South hauled him awkwardly to his feet.

'I wasn't gonna kill you,' the Yankee said. 'Not after you gave me my life this afternoon — but I was gonna take you prisoner.'

The tall man laughed, he couldn't help it.

'What were you gonna do? Feed me? Drag me back to your lines . . . ?'

'Lines? Hell, we're scattered all over the blamed countryside lookin' for you Johnny Rebs. You sure know how to run.'

'You were no slouch the way you took off across the creek this afternoon.'

The man pushed brown hair back from his dripping face and nodded. 'No. I was kinda expectin' a bullet in the back.'

The Reb took great delight in grinning and telling him, 'Wasn't even tempted — seeing as I didn't have any ammo.'

The Yankee stared in disbelief. 'You mean — ? You sayin' that Spencer was — ? I ran when there — ? Well smoke me! If that don't beat all!' He grinned suddenly. 'You son of a bitch! You think fast!'

The Reb shrugged. 'Why're we standing talking in the rain?'

'You're right — found me a jack-rabbit, all skinned and dressed in a meat safe lyin' in the fork of a tree. Must've been blown there by an explosion.'

They sat down close to the fire, protected mostly from the rain, and ate quickly, leaving only bare bones and some of these they even crunched up for the thin strip of marrow. They licked their greasy fingers and each burped, grinned.

'Helluva thing, eh?' the Yankee said. 'Couple hours ago we was tryin' our best to kill each other. Now . . . '

The Southerner looked at him soberly and said quietly, 'I ain't going back.'

'Back where?'

'To the army. I meant it when I said I've had a bellyful. Found the body of one of my pards not long after I came round this afternoon. He was just a kid, barely sixteen. Kinfolk by marriage — only way I recognized him was by the boots he was wearing. I gave 'em to him. No, the War's nearly over. They'll think I'm dead, anyway, died in the bombardment. No one from the army'll be looking for me and I've got family in Louisiana.'

'You're gonna — desert?'

'Walking home is what I'm gonna do. I've given the Confederacy just over four years of my life. It owes me something and there's no point in dying for it now when it's dead itself.'

'I heard Southerners would never give up.'

'I said I figure the South owes me something — I ain't giving up. If the Confederacy suddenly got back on to its feet, came good with all that gold they're s'posed to have had — and misplaced — and could supply guns and food again, I'd take up arms agin the North tomorrow.'

'We'd be enemies again then.' The Yank spoke quietly, with a touch of sadness in his voice.

'Well, we ain't exactly friends now — don't even know each other's names.'

The Northerner hesitated then said, 'You can call me 'Lobo'. They always say I'm lean as a wolf.'

The Rebel smiled. 'I get it — OK. Hawk. I've been told I got eyes like a hawk.'

'Not to mention the nose!' Lobo said it jokingly and thrust out his hand.

'Nice to meet you, Hawk.'

'Likewise.' They gripped and both bemoaned the fact that they didn't even have any tobacco to share.

'Say, talkin' about gold — well, you mentioned it briefly. I used a lotta papers I found lying around in the bank and before you showed up was amusin' myself readin' some before I tossed 'em into the fire.' He rummaged in a pile and brought out a ledger that had had many of its pages ripped out, presumably to feed the fire that was dying slowly now.

Lobo showed Hawk half a torn page.

'Here, see? 'Transfer of gold bars and cash box received 17 March 1865, taken into the bank's vault for safekeeping before shipment to Healyville branch'.' He turned the page towards the fading light. 'And here? The total — only part of a figure but it looks like $200,000 to me . . . '

Hawk stiffened, squinting. His breath hissed through his nostrils. 'It sure does! That date — only two days before we arrived. Did the safe survive the bombardment?'

Lobo sighed soberly. 'It didn't. I found it, all mangled and not a bar of gold in sight.'

'Guess they must've shipped the gold on to the Healyville branch then before the shells started falling.'

'Looks that way. Healyville ain't all that far. So it's likely sittin' in the bank over there with the War windin' down around it and never to be used except for them that's on the spot when the armistice is signed. Be easy to lose the paperwork in all the excitement . . . '

Hawk looked at him sharply. 'If you were on the spot and knew what you were about, yeah. I guess someone'll get rich from it.'

'Could be you and me — and a few likeminded friends.'

'What're you talking about?' Hawk demanded. 'The gold's in a *bank*, man. It'll be guarded, by your side, most likely. Or even if it's Southern gold, there's gonna be a lot of armed men

41

watching over it.'

'Maybe — but what've we got to lose?'

'We?'

'Sure. Dress it up any way you like, but we're nothin' but a couple deserters. They catch us, they'll shoot us. They don't catch us, what've we got? No money, rags on our backs, empty guns, no future . . . me, I'd be willin' to take a chance of gettin' my hands on a few bars of that gold. I ain't greedy. Say five — five bars apiece. They'd be all we could carry anyway, I guess.'

He could see Hawk was thinking about it now. And it didn't take long before he reached a decision.

'Gonna take a heap of planning and we'll need help.'

'I reckon I can find help. It's a deal then?'

He tentatively thrust out his right hand and after a slight hesitation, Hawk gripped with Lobo and the deal was made.

★ ★ ★

It was a good enough plan. Between them, they found half-a-dozen deserters, from both sides, and they got guns and stole horses and made their way to Healyville.

There was a shoot-out with a small detachment of Yankee soldiers left in the town and then the bank was theirs for the taking.

Only thing was, there was nothing to take.

Someone before them had blown the safe — and left a couple of dead men lying nearby as well — and cleaned it out.

If the gold had ever been in there, it wasn't now.

★ ★ ★

Then word of Appomattox filtered down to them and suddenly the men were homesick and they disbanded and went their own ways.

None of them ever expected to see any of the others again.

3

Quest

'I spent best part of a year in Louisiana lookin' for you,' Lobo told Hawk through the bars of the cell.

'You didn't even know my name.'

'No — made it hard. But I think I found your place — called 'Winterset'. Old darkie named Scratch said the folks who owned the place died in the fire that destroyed it. And 'Mr Chris' was killed in New Mexico just before the end of the War . . . '

Hawk's face was grim as he nodded. 'That was the place. A Confederate lieutenant found some cotton bales in the cellar, claimed my folks were aiming to smuggle them to British boats to run the blockade. Tied the folks up and burned the house down around 'em.'

'Jesus! Your own people!'

'Not my people!' snapped Hawk, eyes narrowed. 'Redneck outlaws masquerading as soldiers but looting and murdering all through the south. I tracked down that damn lieutenant eventually.'

Lobo waited expectantly. When Hawk didn't say any more he asked impatiently, 'And . . . ?'

'I killed him. Trouble was, by then he'd switched sides, was helping the Reconstruction. I had to get out of Louisiana in a hurry.'

'And ended here — as a deputy to a sour-gut sheriff.'

Hawk frowned at the man's tone. 'At least I'm on this side of the bars.'

Lobo smiled ruefully. 'That you are. You know that gold?'

'The $200,000 we didn't get?'

'Yeah — well, that was just bad luck. We got there too late. They had me posted as a deserter — dunno how they figured I hadn't been killed at Kettledrum, but I was on the run. Got in with a wild bunch, heard of the men who raided the Healyville bank and got away with the gold.'

'The hell you say!'

Lobo's smile grew wider and he lowered his voice. 'Not only that, I set out to track down some of the gang members — them that was still livin'. An' there was only two.'

Hawk was tense now but he waited patiently for further explanation.

'Two brothers, Mitch and Denny Brackett.'

'Hell, there's wanted dodgers out on them two! Got 'em in the front office, murderin' snakes.'

'Not no more — they're dead. Seems I asked too many questions about that gold and they tried to kill me. I nailed Mitch dead-centre but Denny was only wounded. Body-hit. Mighty painful. Or I made it that way.' He paused to get Hawk's reaction. The man's lean face was hard and watchful but he said nothing. 'Seems there was some cash as well as the gold. The Bracketts got a third of the gold bars as their share and took off. But there was a hint they jumped the others, took the lot, includin' the cash and buried it right here in Colorado.'

'Which covers a helluva lot of territory!'

'Yeah, but — there's a place over the sierras called Pagosa Springs. Once part of an Indian reservation but they moved the Injuns out and broke it up into prove-up quarter-sections.'

'I know it. Long ways from here.'

Lobo's eyes glittered in the lamplight and he gripped the bars. 'By Godfrey, my luck's changin'! When that sheriff threw me in here I figured I was in for another run of bad luck but — you really know Pagosa Springs?'

'Chased some renegades up there a while back.'

'Listen, Hawk — Denny Brackett was convinced he was dyin' and I promised him I'd make it mighty painful for him, so he told me where he and Mitch had buried what was left of their share of the gold. I've got the directions and the landmarks. All I need is a stake and a hoss to get there.' He grinned widely. 'Or a pardner.'

Hawk had seen it coming and didn't show any surprise. 'You want me to quit and ride with you?'

'Well, I know it'd be hard for you to leave such a well-paid job as deputy in a one-horse town like this and who knows when you might find another boss as thoughtful and congenial as Atwater, but — yeah, I'm suggestin' you quit, lemme out, and ride with me. You must have a few bucks saved so's we could get some grub and supplies . . . ?'

'Well, mebbe the job ain't quite as you described, Lobo,' Hawk said sardonically, 'but it *is* work. I quit and what do I get out of it?'

Lobo spread his arms wide. 'Hell, what we always aimed to get outta that gold — split it right down the middle.'

'This Denny gave you all the info you need?'

'And glad to do it.'

There was a lot implied by those few words.

'What happened to him?'

Lobo shrugged. 'I said if he told me what I wanted to know I wouldn't kill him. So I rode out.'

'And left him to die of his wounds.'

'Far as I'm concerned, I kept my word. Well, you interested or not?'

Hawk was interested. He had long been fed-up with Atwater and his petty ways, his low pay and exploitation by the sheriff. But it had been a job with enough pay so that he ate regularly and work of any kind was hard to find in these tough times, especially if you were a Southerner.

He felt that Lobo's offer was a mite suspect, but . . .

'OK,' he said abruptly, turning back down the passage towards the front office. 'I'll get the keys and leave a note for Atwater to take your fine out of the wages he owes me — which I'll never see anyway, but it'll likely keep him from putting out a dodger on us.'

49

'How about mounts?' Lobo called after him.

'I've got one and there's the hoss I brought in that dead outlaw on. Belonged to him so we can take that without being called hoss-thieves. Keep Atwater off our necks.'

Lobo let out a holler that echoed down the passage.

'By Godfrey! At last I'm gonna be rich!'

* * *

They cleared town less than twenty minutes later.

Nobody yelled at them, nobody took any pot-shots, and the lights soon dropped behind as they galloped on into the night.

* * *

By the time they crossed the San Juan Range and found a way over the permanently snow-capped Summit Peak, they

50

had travelled a hundred miles. The horses were weary and trail-shagged, not liking the colder air of the high peak. Low on supplies now, they made night camp just below the summit on the far side and wolves howled in the sparse timber, further upsetting the mounts.

The down-trail was no easier, steep and with many sections where the ground was loose underfoot. It narrowed way down so that when Hawk's black skidded, rocks sailed over the crumbling edge, dropping into the clear air and falling with a clatter down the steep sides. A man wouldn't stand a chance if he went off there.

Lobo wasn't keen on the high trail and said so. 'I lived on the plains in Dakota, kept away from the hills. Got a thing about high places. Makes me feel like I want to jump off and try to fly.'

'Wouldn't recommend it.'

'How much more we gotta go?'

'We'll camp at the bottom tonight — could make the Pagosa Springs area by the next sundown.'

'Don't have to go right into the town — the landmarks are this side of it.'

'Better show me the map.' Hawk said it casually but he had been a mite piqued that Lobo didn't seem to trust him all the way and had kept the rough map he claimed to have to himself.

'We'll go over it when we make camp,' the Yankee said shortly.

It took them most of the day to make the dangerous descent and then Hawk led the way to a tree-lined creek. They camped on a gravel spit that projected into the creek and caught a couple of fish which they cooked in the coals for supper. Their food supplies were low and they would be forced to live off the land while searching for the landmarks Lobo needed. Unless they went into town and spent Hawk's last few dollars. They had taken some ammunition from Atwater's office in Alamosa and it bothered Hawk a little. Knowing the petty kind of man Atwater was, he wouldn't be surprised if the sheriff came after them or even put out a dodger on them.

Lobo's map was crude and had names scrawled on blank sections of the crumpled paper but without any indication of what the landmarks looked like.

'Can't tell much from this!' Hawk said when he saw it. '*Saddleback — Old Man — Lake —* what lake? I don't know of any lakes in the Pagosa neck of the woods. Even the 'Springs' of the name isn't right — it was the site of old Indian tanks in the rocks, but they're said to have dried-up long ago. Saddleback might be the description of a ridge, but what about 'Old Man'?'

Lobo smiled crookedly. 'I know what they look like. Just dunno where they are. Figured I'd have to spend a lot of time lookin' — but you can locate 'em easier.'

'Not unless I know more . . . '

Lobo seemed reluctant but finally said, 'Well, the Saddleback's a ridge like you guessed, but it only looks like a saddle when you come in from the north-west at sundown accordin' to Denny Brackett. The 'Lake' is a mirage: early mornin' mist with the sun hittin' it in a small basin gives it the look of water. 'Old Man' is a rock on a slope that looks like an old man's face with a juttin' nose. When you get it in the right position —'

'For what?'

Lobo looked at him sharply. 'You find the Old Man and from where it looks just right you can line up the Saddleback with his 'nose' and the Lake's to the left. Halfway between is a rockfall that leads up to a ledge — and that's where the Bracketts buried the gold.'

'You said something about two separate lots.'

'Yeah, accordin' to Denny. The others buried their loot nearby, I don't have much info about that except it's in the same general area, but I reckon we'll be able to find it.'

'Why'd they bury it at all?'

Lobo looked away. 'Posses were after

'em, I guess. You'd have to ask the Bracketts.'

'I'm asking you, Lobo, and I think all those directions were a helluva lot for a dying mam. If he was as low as you say, they could be all wrong.'

Lobo stiffened. 'Hadn't thought of that.'

'Or, if you were making things hard for him, he could've told you anything just so you'd ease up.'

Lobo swore. 'Damnit, Hawk! Why you gotta think of these things! I was there! I *know* Denny was tellin' the truth. I could feel it. You help me find these landmarks and we'll soon see.' Then he tensed as if he had thought of something. 'You can find 'em, can't you?'

'I can try — I've got an idea where the Saddleback is but I've never heard of the Lake mirage or the Old Man's head.'

'Aw, one thing I forgot to mention — the Bracketts. They was half-breeds, had kin lived on the reservation when it

55

was operatin' up here. They hid out with 'em from time to time when the Law was huntin' 'em.'

Well, that made it more likely to be pretty accurate, Hawk allowed to himself. But he regarded Lobo much more closely now. A white man who could make a 'breed talk about something like that gold, dying or not, had to be real dedicated to his work . . .

* * *

It took them two days before they found all three landmarks. Then they had to find the position where they all fell into place on Lobo's crude map.

There was quite a distance between the Old Man, the Saddleback and the Lake and they did some hard and hot riding before Hawk found the right place for viewing them together.

He used his field glasses and pointed through the bluish haze that would clear later when the sun rose higher in the cloudless sky. 'That could be the ledge. Seems to be straddling what looks like a rockslide, all jumbled up.'

Lobo took the glasses, changed focus, held them for a long time, breathing shallowly through his mouth.

'That's gotta be it!'

It took almost an hour and a half to reach the basin where the slide was, lifting up a shadowed ridge to a broken ledge that zigzagged across. Starting to climb up on foot so as to rest the horses who were suffering from prolonged riding in such rough country, they heard a distant lowing of cows.

'Must be close to the homesteaders,' opined Hawk and Lobo merely nodded, eager to reach the ledge.

They had a pickaxe and a spade which they had stolen from a ranch before they left the San Luis Valley, Hawk carrying the pick, Lobo the spade. They were sweating and begrimed by the time they reached the ledge and although they were breathing hard, Lobo was too impatient to wait and began pacing out the required number of steps to where Denny Brackett had told him the gold was buried.

It was behind some rocks which Lobo clambered over. Suddenly Hawk heard the spade clang loudly on the sandstone, the sound followed by a searing curse.

'What's wrong?' Hawk asked as he started over the rocks. He paused on the top, looking down.

'Gimme the pick — just look at all them rocks!'

'Been washed down from the slope looks like. We better move 'em first before we start digging.'

But Lobo was impatient and lifted the pick, ready to drive it into the ground between some of the head-sized rocks.

At the same time a rifle cracked and a bullet whined off the slope above their heads.

Two more fast shots had them diving for cover. As the bullets ricocheted and the sounds died away, a voice, distorted by echoes off the slope, called through the fading sound of the gunfire.

'Show yourselves, and your hands better be empty or I'll shoot to kill!'

Just to back up the words, three more fast shots raked the rocks they sheltered behind, striking the slope but ricocheting down into the place where they crouched.

'Judas priest!' gasped Lobo. 'That's some shootin'!'

'Yeah, and if we stay here we're gonna be cut to pieces.' Hawk started to stand. 'Best see what it's all about before we get hurt!'

Lobo swore but reluctantly obeyed and they made their way through the jumble of rocks, and stepped out on to the ledge, hands raised shoulder-high.

A black-haired girl dressed in checked shirt and trousers over which she wore leather chaps, stood up from behind a deadfall, a smoking Winchester repeater with a brass action held confidently in small, gloved hands.

'Now keep those hands up and tell me just what the hell you think you're doing on my land.'

4

The North Spread

'Did Harrigan send you?'

She snapped the question as they came closer, hands still in the air.

'Who's Harrigan?' Lobo asked blankly and she frowned slightly, but the gun barrel didn't waver.

'Lew Harrigan.' She jerked her head to the right. 'He owns the L Bar H, beyond the Jerichos.'

Hawk glanced at the low ridge of mountains and shook his head. 'We come from the north-east, ma'am. Don't know no Harrigan.'

Her brown eyes flashed at him. 'Southerner, eh — and your friend is a Yankee, unless I'm mistaken. Unusual alliance. D'you have names?'

'He's Hawk and I'm Lobo. And I'm from Dakota.' Lobo spoke quickly, somewhat defiantly.

'I'm Mattie North. Those names — are you on the dodge?'

'Risky question to ask a stranger, ma'am,' Hawk pointed out, 'but, no, we're not on the dodge. Looking for work, matter of fact.'

'Then why were you climbing to that ledge?' she snapped. '*My* ledge.'

'Heard cows. Was climbing up to see if there were any riders with 'em when you started shooting.'

She considered that, studying the men suspiciously, obviously not happy with what she saw. They had the mark of drifters and they looked hard — or as if they had been used hardly. If they had served in the army, and they would have at their ages she figured, then that might well explain it.

Arriving at a decision, she said slowly, 'Well, I am looking for another man to help on my spread — but I don't think I can afford to hire two.'

Hawk's eyes slid sideways towards Lobo. 'We like to stick together, ma'am.'

She gave a faint smile and even that small movement of her lips made her seem a little younger. Hawk had figured her age somewhere around the mid-to-late twenties. She seemed to have a deal of confidence and a no-nonsense cast to her.

'So you don't want to split up. You must've formed quite a relationship, north and south.'

'Too bad it ain't happenin' on a bigger scale,' allowed Lobo and she nodded gently, soberly.

'Yes, I suppose so. Oh, all right. I'll take you both on if you can convince me you know something about running cattle . . . ?'

'I'm better with hosses than cows,' admitted Lobo, 'but I've rounded up cows and ridden on two trail herds.'

Her gaze flicked to Hawk and he shrugged. 'I rode with Texas Jack Mannering from Corpus Christi to Sedalia, and I've punched cows in west Texas and along the Border. Not much, I have to admit. Just did it for pocket money so I could get back home to Louisiana when war seemed inevitable. Never quite made it and when I finally walked away from it all it was too late — the old place had burned down and my folks along with it.'

'Then you'd have no love for the north.' There was a query in her voice and she looked from one man to the other.

'Wasn't Yankees that did it,' Hawk told her. 'Renegade Southerners — they're all dead now.'

That seemed to rock her and her eyes narrowed a little. There was concern showing on her face for a moment before she nodded gently and lowered the hammer on the Winchester. But she did not swing the barrel aside.

'Before you definitely take the job, I have to tell you, if it's a peaceful life you're looking for, you may not find it here. Lew Harrigan, who I mentioned earlier, has no love for me and would like to see me fail to prove up.'

Hawk frowned. Judging by the girl's

clothes, working style, sure, but pretty good quality, and the fine looking roan mare she had ground-hitched back at the tree line, and the Winchester which did not come cheap, he would have said she had enough money to help her prove up — or already be at that stage.

'I'm working a full section, six-hundred and forty acres.' It was if she had read his mind. 'Perhaps I took on too much, but — I felt I could handle it and, anyway, I came into a small legacy that will help me out. But the thing is, I started out just with a quarter-section grant, proved up, then, after my legacy came through, applied for three more sections, adjoining my first, naturally. I was granted them just before Lew Harrigan put in a claim for one of the same sections that was between his place and the river — '

'Cut him off from water,' Hawk observed.

'Well, he had one other section that would give him river access, but not flat country he could utilize for grazing right up to the river bank. He tried to buy that piece of land off me but I needed it to give me proper access to the river, or, at least better than what I had originally. Naturally, I wouldn't sell and after his appeal to the Lands Agency was thrown out, I began to have — well, troubles.'

'You or your men?' asked Lobo quietly and she threw him a hard look.

'Both,' she said quietly after a little hesitation. 'I've had a few mysterious things happen to my herds and odd fires in pastures — but two of my men have been beaten up by Harrigan's crew, set up in town so it appeared they started it. They both quit. That's why I'm a little short-handed . . . are you still interested in working for me?'

Lobo hesitated but Hawk said, 'Why not? We've got to eat, and I've never worked at a job yet that didn't have some element of danger — Indians, outlaws, rustlers, feuding neighbours.'

Mattie North was regarding Hawk more closely now. 'Understand this,

Hawk: I'm not hiring you at fighting wages. I'm hiring you to work my spread. By the by, the brand is a single letter 'N' with an arrow-head on the upright stroke — like a compass pointing north . . . '

She flushed a little, seeming slightly embarassed.

'Sounds like a good brand — but easy to running-iron into something else.'

'Yes — it can be changed to the 'H' in L Bar H with a little work,' she admitted. 'So far it hasn't happened that I know of. You've had experience with a running-iron, Hawk?'

He smiled crookedly, shook his head. 'Lately, I've been wearing a deputy's star.' He almost added 'in Alamosa' but stopped himself in time. No sense in giving too much information that could be checked out easily: he still wasn't sure just how Atwater would take his defection and the man was miserable enough to bad-mouth him.

'You, Lobo?'

He knew she was asking what jobs he had had of late, but chose to deliberately misconstrue the question. He shook his head. 'Never used a runnin'-iron, nor toted a badge.'

She waited but he volunteered nothing else. Mattie seemed as if she would ask more but decided to let it go and at last lowered her rifle.

'All right — get your mounts and follow me. I'll show you where my land runs and where the lines are in general — and where Harrigan's place is.'

⋆   ⋆   ⋆

After a good deal of riding, during which time Mattie North showed them her land from high ridges and, once, from a mesa, the two riders dropped back as she led the way down the steep trail.

Lobo moved his horse closer to Hawk's. 'We had a chance to say no back there — would've got us outta

67

there and we could've come back later for the gold.'

Hawk shook his head. 'If she's got her crew looking out for this Harrigan or his men, we'd've been seen and she might not have believed we aren't working for Harrigan this time.'

'What could she've done?'

'Put a bullet in us or run us out of the basin — with orders to her crew to shoot on sight if we came back.' Hawk let that sink in for a moment before adding, 'This way, we've got the run of the place, can find time to get back to that ledge and check out the hiding place. Once we pick up the gold, we hightail it.'

'Ye-ah — I say yeah! We — '

'Keep your voice down!' snapped Hawk as the girl looked around, but he merely waved and she turned back to watching the trail's twists and turns.

Lobo's eyes were glinting now. 'Lucky she never saw that pick and shovel!'

'We'll work at playing cowhands for a

few days or a week to allay any suspicions she might still have, then we'll make time to get up there and grab the gold bars — if they're there.'

Lobo's eyes narrowed. 'They are! I'd bet on it! I tell you that Denny Brackett would've sold me his mother if I'd asked him to at the stage.'

Hawk held up a hand. 'I don't want to know,' he said shortly and they rode on after the girl.

★   ★   ★

She had three men working for her: Darkie Dunbar who seemed to be the top hand, not quite at foreman status, a dried-out ranny in his mid-thirties, sober and taciturn; Tallon, a rawboned rider who liked to whistle softly a few annoying bars of some obscure song that always sounded out of tune to Hawk; and the third man was called simply Purdy. He seemed like an average, easy-going rider who cheerfully removed all his gear from a lower bunk for Lobo, tossing his possessions in an untidy heap in one corner.

They were all Yankees and Dunbar, in particular, watched Hawk closely until the tall man asked mildly,

'Something you want to say, Dunbar?'

'Yeah — for a start you can call me 'Darkie' or 'Mister Dunbar'. And mostly it'd make me happy if you keep your goddamn mouth mostly closed.' He made a spitting motion on the bunkhouse floor. 'Caint abide that Southern-fried accent.'

'You'll get used to it,' Hawk said and Dunbar stepped forward, the others going silent, watching closely.

Dunbar shook his head. 'No — I won't get used to it. Don't aim to even try to get used to it. You just do what I tell you an' we'll get along fine.'

'Doubt that.'

Dunbar stiffened. 'Listen, I said keep your mouth shut!'

'Just like I said, I doubt we'll get along . . . and, just so we savvy each other, Dunbar, I'll talk when I need to or when I want to.' He met and held Dunbar's chilled gaze, spread his hands and added, 'If you don't like it, of course . . . '

The words hung in the air, a plain challenge. Dunbar's face darkened even more as blood flushed under his swarthy skin and his fists clenched down at his sides. He started forward when they heard the sound of an iron triangle being beaten with a metal rod outside.

Tallon licked his lips and said, 'That's the supper bell, Darkie. You know how she don't like us to be late at table.'

Dunbar scowled but Hawk had the notion he was glad enough to have an excuse not to have to start something.

'Aaah! You'll keep, Hawk!' he growled and stormed out.

The others followed.

'Nice friendly place,' opined Lobo as they went out the door.

Hawk smiled slowly. 'We'll see.'

★ ★ ★

A week passed without any further overt trouble from Dunbar but the man was surly and ignored Hawk as much as he could. Hawk worked easily and unworriedly. If Dunbar wanted to push things into a fight that was OK by him — if not, it was still OK and what he would prefer.

There weren't many cattle branded as yet and the girl explained:

'When the Indians were moved off the reservation land all the mavericks in the Jericho Hills and from as far away as the foothills of the San Juans scattered and moved in this general direction. Most of the homesteaders have tried to build up their herds by rounding up some of the mavericks and brush cattle while they used what little money they have for proving up on their sections — building a house and barns and fences and so on. I've done it and while I'm in a position now to buy a few cows to enlarge my herd, I still rope in any mavericks I can. But I've been concentrating on proving up on those last three sections — the sooner I do it, the sooner Harrigan will leave me alone.'

'How you figure that?' Hawk asked sceptically.

She spread her hands as if it should be self-evident. 'He has nothing to gain once I've proved up and been granted tenure of the land.'

Hawk pursed his lips and said slowly, 'From the little you've told me about Lew Harrigan, I'd say he's not a man who'll give up that easy.'

She frowned. 'I think he will — and I'm in a better position to make judgement than you, Hawk.'

He took the reprimand and figured it was none of his business anyway. Once he and Lobo had the gold they would light a shuck and forget all about Mattie North and her troubles . . .

A day or so later, he found himself tracking a couple of cows — branded or not, he didn't yet know — and the trail led over towards the Jerichos. It was a blustery day and he wished he had a slicker but the showers of rain hadn't been too heavy and so far his clothing, though damp, was not too uncomfortable.

He rode in through brush, had trouble finding the tracks, and paused under a rock overhang to roll a cigarette. He was about to strike the vesta on his thumbnail when he heard the unmistakable bawling of a cow being branded. That plaintive, pain-filled sharp bellow edged with shock, followed by a couple of lesser bawls.

He put the unlit cigarette into his shirt pocket and heeled the black forward. There was a small cutting through the hills and he figured the sound had come from beyond the far end.

He rode through almost to the end, dismounted and reached for the Henry in the saddle scabbard.

'Leave that gun on the saddle!' a voice growled from above him and he snapped his head up.

A man stood on a narrow ledge, feet planted firmly, covering him with a rifle. He was dressed in sweat-stained range clothes, wore a drooping *pistolero* moustache, his beefy shoulders filling his denim shirt to straining point.

'What the hell you think you're doin'?'

Hawk let the Henry slide back into the scabbard and stepped back from his horse, holding his hands out from his sides. 'Heard a cow bawling and was coming to take a look-see.'

'This is Harrigan land, mister, and you don't work for L Bar H so that makes you a trespasser.' The man lifted the rifle. 'Usually we shoot 'em on sight — 'specially if they come from the direction of the North spread. You one of them new cowhands she's hired?'

'Name's Hawk.'

The man grunted. 'Yeah — the Johnny Reb. Heard about you. I killed me a whole slew of Rebs durin' the War.'

'Likely as many Yankees that I killed, but so what? War's over now.'

The man scoffed. 'Well, you figure that way, I'm right surprised you've lived so long.' The rifle barrel jerked. 'Walk on through. You try anythin' and . . .'

He didn't have to complete the threat and Hawk walked the rest of the way through the cutting, the man pacing him on the slope and coming down behind him as they cleared the walls. The rain had stopped now and the wind had dropped. They were in a large draw with some brush and a few boulders. Four or five men were working a bunch of cows from a rope corral. There was a branding fire and Hawk watched them throw down a cow, one kneeling and holding the thrashing forelegs, another sitting on the hind-quarters, while a third man went to work with a heated iron. Hawk knew instinctively the man was using a running-iron, blotting out features of the original brand and then reaching for a second iron to overlay the new markings.

Hawk looked at the man with the moustache. 'They're not mavericks you're branding.'

'No — North spread stuff. Wandered on to my land.'

Hawk snapped his head up. 'You're Harrigan?' The man nodded and rifle-urged him forward. 'You try that down in Texas and they'd lynch you.'

Harrigan chuckled. 'We're not down in Texas. Cows wander on to my land, I claim 'em. I make my own law.'

'It's rustling.'

The rifle barrel jabbed painfully against Hawk's spine, bringing a gasp from him as he staggered. He started to turn around and the rifle barrel clipped him hard enough to knock off his hat. Harrigan thrust him forward and the men at the branding fire and the corral looked curiously at their boss.

'The Johnny Reb from North — reckons they'd string us up down in

Texas for changin' brands like we're doin'.'

The man who had wielded the hot irons walked across, tugging his stained and scorched workgloves tighter on to big hands. He glanced at Harrigan.

'New man, eh, boss? Looks like he's gotta find out how things are round here.'

'Well, he sure don't seem to savvy how we work things on L Bar H, Tip — calls himself Hawk.'

'Texas Hawk, huh?' the big man said with a leer, still tugging at his gloves.

'I'm from Tennessee.'

Tip O'Malley shrugged the heavy shoulders. 'Texas, Tennessee, what's the difference? They're both full of Southern trash.'

Hawk said nothing, tensing himself for what he knew was inevitably coming. O'Malley glanced at Harrigan and the rancher must have nodded. Tip was tugging his right glove tightly down between his thick fingers when suddenly it snapped forward, moving no more than eight inches.

Hawk's head snapped back and he staggered several paces before his feet tangled and he went floundering on to one knee. By that time O'Malley had stepped in, and brought a knee up into his face, stretching him out on the ground.

It was the worst place to be in this situation. The other men moved in with O'Malley and boots thudded into Hawk as he tried to cover his head with his arms, draw up his knees. He rolled and twisted but they kept after him and he knew he couldn't take much more without passing out. Desperately, he scooped up a handful of gravel and flung it into the leering, sweating faces.

As they staggered back, instinctively stopping to protect their eyes, he kicked one in the kneecap and heard him howl as the man danced away on one leg. He thrust upright, grunting in pain, off-balance, but knowing this was the only chance he was going to get. He punched someone in the nose, missed with a wild swing and felt O'Malley's work-stiffened gloves slam into his kidneys. His legs wanted to fold but he willed them to support him a little longer. He turned and grabbed O'Malley's shirtfront, pulling the man in violently and snapping his head forward, laying his forehead across the man's nose.

O'Malley howled but as he went to move back, Hawk retained his grip on the shirt and brought up his knee. Tip was wise in the ways of rough-and-tumble and instinctively turned sideways, taking much of the power of the lifting knee on his thigh. But the knee reached his groin just the same and he went down.

But it was too late for Hawk to take much pleasure in that fact. Harrigan slammed him across the back of the head with the rifle butt and he fell, spiralling through blackness that swiftly grew deeper and deeper.

Even before he had hit the ground and stretched out he felt their boots driving into his unprotected body.

5

Whose Gold?

Lobo had been trying all week to get back to Rockslide Ledge, as he learned that was what the cowhands of North ranch called the place where the gold was buried.

He was impatient and it had made him irritable and snappy and he and Dunbar had come close to trading punches, only Mattie North herself had intervened.

'Damnit, I didn't aim to go back to forty-and-found!' Lobo griped to Hawk when they were alone. 'I aimed to pick up that gold and live it up, or if there was enough to settle someplace and work for *myself*. I'm through workin' for wages soon as we dig up the gold.'

'Just watch it,' Hawk had warned. 'Dunbar doesn't trust either of us and

I'm not even sure the girl does, either. We're in no hurry. You're sure it's buried there so it'll be there when we finally make our move.'

But that wasn't good enough for Lobo.

Dunbar ordered him to ride the river and check for floating logs as they were thinking of throwing up a small weir to divert water into one of the pastures, and he didn't want old trees crashing down on it before it was built.

Lobo gave it a cursory check by riding up to a rise that looked out over North land to the river. He had neglected to bring field glasses with him but he couldn't see much debris floating out there. That was a good enough check for him. He dropped down off the rise and rode full tilt for Rockslide Ledge.

He clambered up the slide to where they had left the shovel and pick but before he started digging, he climbed a little higher, just to make sure Dunbar or the others weren't around and likely to ride in and surprise him.

No, no sign of them. He started to clamber back down when a movement out of the corner of his eye drew his attention. It was way out on the plain between this ridge and the Jericho foothills. He swore. *A rider!* Cursing the luck he climbed higher again for a better view, flattening himself atop a boulder, wishing more than ever for the field glasses now.

He squinted, shading his eyes, frowning. Something was wrong with that rider out there . . . kind of slumped, swaying from side to side on the big black horse. *Black horse!* His skin prickled. *Hawk rode the only black horse he had seen around here . . .*

He stashed the shovel and pick again, slid recklessly down and hit the saddle of his blue at a run, the gold momentarily forgotten.

★ ★ ★

When Lobo drew closer his apprehension increased swiftly, recognizing Hawk's clothes and realizing the man was roped in his saddle.

He'd seen men sent home like that before . . .

He called out as he spurred the blue in close but there was no response and by then he saw the torn clothing and the blood on the fluttering rags.

'Judas priest!' he hissed, reining down alongside.

He lifted Hawk's face and was surprised to find it wasn't all that bad — sure there was torn flesh, dried snakes of blood and bruising, with one eye swollen, but the man seemed to have sustained most of his injuries on his body.

Through the torn clothing, he could see the heavy bruising and bloody flesh and he knew Hawk would be lucky not to have a set of broken ribs. To help prevent making any such damage any worse, he took his lariat and awkwardly wound it round and round Hawk's torso from waist to armpits. Hawk moaned and snapped his head up once or twice but he was unconscious the whole time.

'That'll hold you, pard,' Lobo gritted and then proceeded to lead Hawk's mount back away from the Jerichos, riding slowly.

It took several hours to reach the ranch at the walking pace, but he didn't want any ragged ends of broken ribs rubbing together and snapping off in little splinters that could work into the lungs and rupture them.

Purdy was working on the barn and climbed down from his ladder when he saw Lobo coming in, calling to Mattie. The blood drained from her face when she recognized another of her riders who had been beaten up by Harrigan's crew.

'Bring him into the house,' she called to Purdy and Lobo, then hurried back inside to prepare medications and hot water.

* * *

It was just on daylight before Hawk came round enough to actually know where he was and to speak lucidly. Twice before he had opened his eyes and muttered a few words, but he had still been confused and dazed.

This time he looked around the dimly-lit room, he was surprised to find Mattie North dozing in a high-backed chair on one side of the bed. She must have sensed he was awake for she started, blinked, yawned but stopped the motion halfway when she saw him staring at her.

Quickly she rose and leaned over him. 'Don't try to move — you don't have any broken ribs, by some miracle, but they are certainly bruised and they'll hurt for some time.'

'I — b'lieve you,' he gasped, grimacing. 'Your — house?'

His eyes rolled, indicating the room.

'Spare room, never used. Is the pain bad?'

He hesitated, then nodded slightly. 'Nothing a shot of whiskey can't help.'

She smiled thinly. 'Well, that's all it'll do — help a little.' But she left the room and came back with a shot glass of good whiskey and held his throbbing head while he sipped it. The fire spread through him but he had to admit he didn't feel much better for it.

'Tell me what happened.'

He did, in fits and starts, ending with, 'I know they used a running-iron on at least three of your cows — wasn't in very good shape for an accurate count.'

Her mouth was drawn into a tight line. 'It's happened before, but Tip O'Malley is so good with a running-iron that once the brand is changed, it's hard to tell.'

'There a sheriff in town?'

'No — no real law west of the San Juans. The army come in now and again to settle disputes but they come when it suits them. I've tried before to get them here but they work to their own schedule.'

'So Harrigan can steal you blind if something isn't done.'

She sighed. 'That's about the size of it, I'm afraid.'

'Dunbar's always mouthing off about how tough he is. Why don't you call his bluff, send him in to stop Harrigan.'

'It's obvious you still don't know just how rough and tough Lew Harrigan is — despite what he's done to you.'

'I've had worse beatings.' Then he smiled faintly with his swollen lips barely moving. 'Can't rightly recollect when, but . . .'

'At least your spirits seem in good enough shape.'

'Sure — I'll recover. Then I'll settle with Tip O'Malley and Harrigan or anyone else wants to buy in.'

Mattie frowned, staring hard at him. 'I know I have a fight on my hands, Hawk, but I don't want an all-out war.'

'Only way it can go unless it's

somehow stopped dead.'

'You — think you're the man to do that?'

He started to shrug but it hurt too much and he stopped quickly. 'Know I won't stand still for this beating.'

'Not even if I order you to let it ride . . . ?'

'I never have followed stupid orders — even in the army.'

She didn't like that and said coolly, 'That must have gotten you into a deal of trouble.'

'Some — we were what they called an 'Independent Company', which meant we more or less did whatever we figured we could get to work to harass the enemy — '

'Well, if you want to stay at North, you'll obey my orders.'

'I dunno that I want to stay on that bad.'

Their gazes locked and she was holding in her anger but he didn't flinch from it. She knew she had met someone as stubborn as she was herself. *Maybe it's all to the good — she had been going a little soft lately, cutting corners, walking around trouble she should have faced up to . . .*

'Well, you stay put until those ribs are healed before you go planning any revenge. Meanwhile, I believe you are more or less at my mercy.'

She gave him a tight, cold smile and turned and left the room.

★ ★ ★

Lobo came to see him in the afternoon and right away Hawk knew something was wrong. The man's face was tight and he was obviously edgy as Mattie showed him in.

He nodded jerkily, made a few inane remarks, impatient for the girl to leave. Finally she did, saying she would come back with fresh bandages and she would rub more arnica into Hawk's bruises.

As the door closed behind her, Lobo leaned close.

'I managed to get out to that ridge this mornin'.'

'Good — how many bars did you find?'

Lobo looked down at him dully. 'Nary a one. Someone'd been there before, cleaned out the hole and filled it in again. Sign's plain as the nose on your face.' He straightened. 'We been had, Hawk!'

It was difficult to tell just what Hawk was thinking because the bruising had spread across his face, distorting his features. But Lobo frowned and said,

'You don't seem surprised!'

'No — but I think I know where the gold is. Where it went, anyway.'

Just then Mattie came back into the room, and after a while she made it plain that it was time for Lobo to return to his chores and he stomped out angrily. She arched her eyebrows and looked at Hawk puzzledly as she gently painted arnica on to a swelling above his right eye.

'What's wrong with him?'

'Maybe you're working him too hard.'

She scoffed at that suggestion. 'When you feel up to it, I'd like to talk to you about my herds. I think I should buy in some cows, ready-branded, range-bred, not like these shaggy critters we've been rounding up around here. That might make it harder for Harrigan to use his running-iron. They'd be such a superior-looking animal that he'd find it hard to argue if I was to claim such a cow as belonging to me.'

He nodded gently. 'Yeah — well, I wouldn't mind talking it over.'

'You think it's a good idea then?'

'Dunno about that, but I wouldn't mind talking about buying in some good cattle. It would depend on how much you've got to spend, I reckon.'

He was watching her closely and she seemed uncomfortable, started gathering her bandages and jars and said shortly,

'Well, we'll leave it until you feel

more up to it. I'll have to go start supper now.'

He had a feeling she was glad to get out of the room and he smiled slightly, nodding to himself.

'I thought so,' he murmured.

6

Wait

Lobo was impatient. And frustrated. Not to mention mad as hell that someone had beaten him to the buried gold.

Dunbar told him to ride on down to the river this time and check properly for debris floating by, to time the intervals between big trees or logs or dead animals or whatever and mark it down in the book he gave Lobo.

'Take this, too,' he said, handing Lobo a cheap tin watch. The case was scratched and battered and the glass had a large crack running from side to side. 'Keeps pretty good time, good enough anyway to do the job you're s'posed to do. You foul it up this time and you walk.'

Lobo scowled as he put notebook,

pencil and watch into his saddle-bag. 'Maybe I'll walk anyway.'

Dunbar gave him a crooked smile. 'I give you my word you won't be missed!'

Lobo mounted and rode out, swinging around his horse's head so sharply that Dunbar, cursing, had to jump back. He rode out of the yard and Mattie North, finishing her morning cup of coffee on the porch, watched him go.

'You two are heading for trouble.'

'Glad to oblige him anytime.'

'No — I have enough to worry about without fighting among my own men. Try to get along better, Darkie — you're too touchy.'

He scowled but said nothing.

'I want Tallon and Purdy up in the brush behind the hogback today. I was riding yesterday and saw several cows. Bring them down and slap the North brand on them,' she said.

Dunbar nodded and went back towards the bunkhouse, yelling for the cowhands. Mattie tossed the dregs of her coffee over the rail and turned back into the house. Time to wake Hawk and see how he was feeling today.

He was coming on surprisingly well, yet was another source of potential worry. She could see he was brooding about having been beaten up and she wondered if she was going to be able to head him off from going after Tip O'Malley and Harrigan once he was up and around again.

She was tempted to turn him loose, but . . .

★   ★   ★

Lobo spent a couple of hours watching the river, bored and uninterested. There wasn't much debris coming down. In fact the water was pretty clean which meant there hadn't been a lot of rain back in the hills to bring down any dangerous washaways.

But he made a few entries and then his impatience got the better of him and he put away his notebook and the old watch and mounted his horse.

He was going back to the rockslide to take a really good look around this time. He had been so mad when he had discovered there was no gold that he had flung down his pick and shovel and ridden hell for leather back to the ranch to tell Hawk. Now he wanted to see just what he could find in the way of clues that might tell him at least roughly *when* the gold had been taken and — with a little luck — even *who*, or at least something that would point him in the right direction. He had been thinking about that gold for so long that in his mind it was *his* — well, his and Hawk's — and he didn't aim to pass it up without making some effort to find it.

It wasn't far to the Rockslide Ledge and he ground-hitched his mount and clambered up to where he had hidden the pick and shovel. He had left the hole open: he had been so damn mad and in a hurry to tell Hawk the news that he had just stashed the tools and ridden for the ranch.

The bottom of the hole was now covered by a layer of wrinkled and cracked clay. The earth had been moist when he had dug down and he had figured it was because of rains a few days before or even longer. Now he squatted in the hole and examined the clay closely. The sun had dried it out mostly since he had exposed it and he squatted there on his hams, just letting his eyes rove slowly over every inch of it.

He didn't find anything much in the very bottom, except his own mish-mash of footprints, but off to one side and a foot or so above the clay, he found a kind of skid-mark where someone had slipped, perhaps while bending over to lift out a bar of gold. It had been preserved by loose earth when the finder had filled in the hole again, not taking a lot of trouble with the chore. Remaining damp, it had now dried after he had exposed that section of the hole and left it open for a couple of days.

The mark had been made by a riding boot, he was sure of that, and —

'The hell you tryin' to do? Dig your way to China?'

Lobo swung so fast, reaching for his pistol, that he floundered in the bottom of the hole and then as his hand closed over the butt of the gun he froze, hearing the unmistakable sound of a rifle hammer cocking.

There was a man standing at the lip of the hole, covering him with a rifle, a black haloed silhouette against the sun. But Lobo recognized the voice.

Dunbar.

'What you hidin' in there?' Dunbar demanded.

'Nothin' — just found the hole dug and wondered what the hell had been in it.'

Slowly, experimentally, Lobo stood an inch at a time, watching Dunbar's finger that was curled around the trigger of the rifle. The top hand allowed Lobo to straighten up and then jerked his gun barrel, indicating that

Lobo should raise his hands.

Lobo compromised by lifting his hands away from his side and the holstered pistol.

'Just as well I decided to come check on you — was headin' for the river when I seen your mount ground-hitched down there. Now, I want to know what the hell you think you're doin'? We don't pay you for findin' a hidey-hole where you can sleep 'til it's time to go back to the spread.' He bared his teeth. 'B'lieve I warned you if you didn't do a good job you'd be fired. So consider yourself fired!'

'Well, long as I'm not workin' for you anymore.'

Lobo had worked his boot under the handle of the spade and now lifted the leg sharply, bringing the tool with it. It struck the barrel of Dunbar's rifle and the man staggered back as the weapon discharged, the shot echoing through the hills.

Lobo came out of the hole like a wild pig protecting its young, arms reaching for Dunbar's lower legs, head butting the man in the stomach. Together they rolled down the slope and before they reached the bottom, Lobo broke free and fought to find his feet. Dunbar rolled all the way to the bottom of the slide and was just getting up, staggering, when Lobo's body hurtled through the air and hit him full force.

Again, both men hit the ground and dust rose and gravel flew as they scrabbled to get in a blow or to find the upper position. But they bucked and grunted and rolled and kneed, drove elbows into ribs and faces and backs, swung punches so wild that only about one in four connected and then because of the awkwardness of the position the blow lacked impact.

They kicked apart and rolled and stumbled to their feet, filthy, clothes ripped, some blood showing, and some skin scraped raw. They paused only briefly, then with bared teeth and guttural curses, they ran at each other, hitting like a couple of bighorn sheep at mating time. Their bodies shuddered with the impact and for a few moments both men were too stunned and breathless to start swinging. But then the moment passed and Lobo ducked a driving right, slammed one of his own under Dunbar's ribs and had the satisfaction of seeing the man's boots leave the ground as he grunted loudly and stumbled back. Lobo went after him but his boot slipped on the gravel and he fell to one knee.

Before he could straighten, Dunbar stepped in and hooked him on the side of the neck. Searing pain leapt through Lobo and down his right arm. There was a blinding flash and from out of the middle of that flash came a fist, headed straight for his jaw. He managed to twist aside and duck his head but the blow still slammed into him like a pile-driver and he went down, one hand reaching out to keep from falling all the way.

Dunbar bared his teeth and ran in, kicking. Lobo rolled with it but his body still shook with the impact of the boot skidding across his lower ribs. He slammed down with his hand to push the leg away, grabbed the greasy trousers instead, and yanked violently. Dunbar yelled as his leg shot up into the air and he lifted off the ground, crashing down on his back. Lobo was on him in a flash.

He dropped knee-first on to Dunbar's chest and the breath exploded from the man and he seemed to fold in upon himself. Lobo back-handed him twice, straddled the dazed man, twisted fingers in the sweaty, dark hair and pounded the man's head into the ground. Dunbar was almost out when Lobo held him clear of the ground with his left hand and hammered three mauling rights into the slack face.

The nose broke and the lips mashed and Dunbar's head lolled limply to one side. Lobo kept pounding him a few more times, shook him violently, and then let him collapse to the ground.

Dunbar's head rapped hard but he

didn't move, just lay there, air snorting through his bubbling, smashed nose.

Lobo fell sprawling as he tried to lift his leg across the man's body and, fighting for breath, feeling his hurts as he spat some blood, crawled to the shade of a boulder. He leaned his aching shoulders against it, tilting back his head, feeling the warmth of the sun on his battered face.

He closed his eyes with a tired sigh.

* ★ *

'What're you doing in here?'

Hawk, leaning on the desk in the small room used as a ranch office, glanced up sharply, still holding the paper he had been reading when Mattie North came in. She didn't give him a chance to answer, strode swiftly across the room and snatched the paper from his hand, glaring.

'I was looking for something to read,' he said mildly, still leaning on the desk for a measure of support.

'So you read my private papers!'

'Didn't mean to pry — just saw them lying there and it had something about your land. I've never seen a prove up homestead paper before and I was just curious.'

'You know what happened to the proverbial cat who became curious!'

He smiled thinly. 'I'm sorry.'

She was breathing fast and folded the paper, becoming more angry when she didn't fold it back along the original lines. She fought it stubbornly until she had it right and shook it in his face.

'Did you find out what you wanted to know?'

'Not really — but I did get the notion that you're not eligible for land grant if you have more than a certain amount of money . . . ' He waited. She said nothing, only looked steadily at him. 'Just wondered that if you've got enough to buy cattle, it might make you — ineligible.'

'It may — that's why I have to spread out what I spend. If I spend too much too quickly they'll want to know where the money came from and I could lose the land.'

'That — legacy you came into must've caused you some worry then.'

Her eyes narrowed, but there was anxiety there as well as dwindling anger. 'Ye-es. It was from an uncle I hardly knew. Back in Springfield, Illinois.'

'You didn't declare it?'

'I — didn't have to. It was paid — well, in cash, or as good as, I suppose.'

'You mean like jewellery you could sell — or gold?'

He was watching for it so he saw the flash of fear flare behind her eyes and although she hid it quickly, there was not much she could do to stop the blood draining from her face. She went white at the mention of 'gold'.

'Who are you, Hawk?' she countered, but her voice wasn't quite as steady as usual.

'From Tennessee originally, grew up

mostly in Louisiana when we moved there because of some damn feud — I was too young to remember much about that. Got restless in my early teens, left the small plantation Pa managed to build up and went a'drifting. Fought in the War till I'd had enough just a few weeks before it ended, dumped my uniform and went drifting again, which wasn't so easy with Reconstruction but I did some trail-driving and ranch work down in Texas. Took a deputy's badge in Alamosa before coming here.' He paused, gaze steady, and he saw she was finding it difficult to hold her eyes on his face. Then he added quietly, 'Came looking for some gold I'd heard was buried here-abouts.'

She stiffened. 'Where d'you mean — 'here-abouts'?'

He shrugged, swaying a little, still stiff and sore. 'On land that used to be part of an Indian reservation — part of your spread, actually.'

'So you were looking for the gold

when I found you and Lobo! I knew it!'

He smiled. 'Now why would you think that? Unless you knew there was gold buried on that ridge.'

'Don't be ridiculous!' she snapped. 'How could I?'

'Could've come across it accidentally — like after rain, some more of that rockslide washed away, maybe enough to show one of the bars . . . that the way it happened, Mattie? Just a piece of sheer luck. A washaway, sun striking the end or side of a gold bar . . . ?'

She walked slowly around the desk and sat down heavily in the chair. Her hands had worked on the homestead deed and crumpled it and she started to smoothe it in nervous reaction, then simply tossed it on to the desktop.

'So — you're claiming it as your gold?'

'We-ell, I'd like to but I guess it was up for grabs.' He told her briefly how he and Lobo came to know about the gold and she seemed more relaxed afterward.

'I thought it might've been outlaw gold or some buried by the Confederacy — their markings are stamped all over the bars. There were only four bars there. Nowhere near the $200,000 you mentioned.'

'No — it was split up with the rest of the wild bunch who stole it after Healyville. There was supposed to be some cash money, too.'

She waited and then sat back and spread her hands.

'Well — what do we do now?'

'How many bars d'you have left?'

He thought she wasn't going to answer but finally, she said, 'Three.'

'Could share fifty-fifty.'

'Why should I do that?'

He shrugged. 'Lobo and I came down here looking to make our fortune — but not by working for forty-and-found.'

'You have no more right to that gold than I do!' Then she smiled wryly. 'Except I have it now, so that gives me a big advantage.'

He nodded, admitting that. 'Lobo's gone out to look for it. He's already mighty disappointed at finding just an empty hole. When he gets back — '

She tossed her head. 'I believe you're threatening me!'

'I was about to say when he gets back we'd best, all three of us, sit down and talk about it.'

After a while she said, 'What's there to talk about? I beat you to the gold, and I believe earlier you mentioned the words 'finders keepers'?'

Hawk hitched an aching hip on to a corner of the desk, a sigh coming out of him: he still felt as if he had been dragged by a horse through a boulder field. He looked down at her steadily.

'If the Reconstruction heard about Confederate gold being exchanged for cash or for buying cattle . . . ' He let the rest hang.

'You wouldn't!' she breathed, and he spread his hands helplessly. Her lips compressed. 'Perhaps the Reconstruction would be interested to hear there are a couple of deserters in the vicinity, too.'

'They might be — but this is a kind of Mexican stand-off, ain't it?'

The door was thrown open and suddenly the battered Lobo was standing there, wild-eyed and dusty, as he said, 'It don't have to be! We can just take the gold and go — what can she do about it? Complain to the Reconstruction and get herself into a helluva lot of trouble explainin' how she came by the gold in the first place and didn't declare it? Hell, Hawk, you're too slow on the uptake — we're the ones in the saddle here . . . and the sooner we move the better.'

7

Gold for the Taking

Grunting a little with the movement of the saddle, Darkie Dunbar spat another piece of broken tooth as he approached the ranch. He was sick and sore. Who the hell would ever have thought that damn Lobo could fight like a sackful of wildcats?

It was the worst beating Dunbar had taken in many a day. But maybe it was worth it. At least he had fired the son of a bitch before he had been beaten to a jelly —

'*What the hell!*'

Dunbar reined in as he cleared the hogback and the ranch yard came into full view. He squinted, still not believing his eyes, half-stood in the stirrups.

'Well, goddamnit to hell!' he said aloud, still staring, feeling his heart rate increase.

Where did that bastard get the gall to show up back here after being fired!

He recognized Lobo's horse left with trailing reins down by the corrals. He would have thought the man was a long way away by now. Instead, he was back here — why? He had little or no gear, carried his worldly possessions in his worn saddle-bags.

'Up at the house!' he gritted, stopping his mount behind the barn and dismounting stiffly. He eased his Colt pistol in his holster, frowning. *What the hell was Lobo up to? What kind of a story was he telling Mattie North? And his pard, Hawk . . . ?*

Dunbar made his way around the barn to the corner closest to the house and then ran in an awkward crouch to the end of the porch, waited, listening. He heard the sound of voices coming from the ranch office and, still crouching, made his way beneath the open window.

He heard his own name mentioned and his hand tightened on his pistol . . .

* * *

Hawk and Mattie were both surprised at Lobo's entrance and now Hawk saw his pard's injuries.

'You run into Tip O'Malley, too?'

Lobo smiled wryly. 'Darkie Dunbar — we had what you might call a diff-i-culty.' He dabbed a corner of his mouth that was still bleeding slightly. 'Never mind him — let's get back to the gold.' He set his gaze on the pale-faced girl. 'I reckon she found it — that 'legacy' she mentioned. There's a mark in the clay up there that'd about fit her ridin' boot.'

'Yeah, she stumbled on it,' Hawk said. 'More or less admitted it. Thing is she's got it. How do we get it?'

Lobo's face was hard and Mattie shivered a little, involuntarily, under his gaze. 'She's a woman. All the hands are out on the range.'

'Come on, Lobo!' snapped Hawk. 'We don't need the gold that badly.'

'Who says?'

'I say.' Hawk's voice was flinty and even in his beat-up state he looked mighty menacing.

'Well, then, it's your move — and I don't care which way you jump, long as we end up with the gold.'

Hawk said quietly, watching the girl now. 'Maybe we can split it — '

'No!' snapped Lobo instantly. 'Look, when you get right down to it, that gold is mine! I'm the one found the records of it and so on — I got it out of Denny Brackett where he buried it. I'm bettin' she's already spent it.'

'Only what I needed to,' Mattie said, speaking for the first time in a long while. There was defiance in her face. 'I found it, Lobo, whether you learned of its existence in the first place or not. I need some to help me with the ranch.'

'Heard Hawk say you spend too much and you're gonna have to explain how come, and you'll lose the land grant because you've got too much money.' He winked. 'We'll do you a favour, take the gold off your hands.'

'To put it bluntly, Lobo — you can go to hell!'

Lobo grinned at Hawk. 'Feisty, huh? Mattie, we've got you over a barrel and you know it. Quit stallin' — OK, we'll split with you. How much is left?'

'Three bars — I — I wasn't game to spend any more.'

'One bar apiece then,' Lobo said and as she started to protest, he said to Hawk, 'Bit less than the five we planned on but better'n nothin'.'

'That's not fair!'

'Lady, I'm way past bein' 'fair' when it comes to that gold.' Lobo had a challenging look on his face now, watching Hawk closely. 'Don't you go soft on me, Hawk, *amigo*! I've come a long way on this deal, had a tougher time than you. It's a bar apiece or I take the lot.'

She curled a lip, looking at Hawk. 'Some partner you have!'

'He had it rougher'n me,' Hawk allowed. 'He's entitled to call the tune.'

'Well, you have nothing to lose, do you!'

'You've had the use of one bar and you'll have another. Double what we get.'

'This could go on forever,' snapped Lobo. 'It's decided. Now you take us to the gold and we'll be on our way, Mattie.'

Her nostrils were white and pinched, her lips compressed. Then she smiled slowly. 'That's the chink in your armour, Lobo, isn't it? You don't know where it's hidden.'

Hard-faced, Lobo walked across to the desk, scooped up the glass oil lamp and lifted it in his left hand, ready to throw. His right hand fumbled a vesta out of his shirt pocket and he held it up, thumbnail against the brown head.

He didn't have to say anything.

She was milk white again, eyes wide. She glanced at Hawk but while he was frowning slightly he made no move to stop Lobo. Her shoulders slumped.

'All right! Damn the both of you! I'll go get it.'

'*We'll* go get it,' Lobo said, setting

the lamp down on the desktop.

'No — you don't need to know exactly where it's hidden except it's in the barn. I'll bring it to you.'

'Sure — that's OK,' Hawk said as Lobo started to protest. He nodded to the girl and she hurried out of the room.

'How the hell we know there're only three bars left?' asked Lobo and Hawk shrugged.

'There's no point in her trying to hold out, Lobo. She says it's in the barn. We could tear it apart in half an hour and find it anyway.'

'Aaah! You're too damn trustin', said so all along.'

'Relax and roll a smoke while we're waiting.'

Hawk took the makings from a shirt pocket and tossed the sack and papers to his pard. Lobo caught them deftly, gave him a sober look then grinned.

'OK — we'll do it your way.'

* * *

It was gloomy in the barn even with one door partly open, but Mattie went straight for the grain bin at the rear of the chunky building, lifted the lid, rolled up her sleeves and began to dig down into the grain.

In a few minutes she had the three gold bars stacked on the floor at her feet and was just straightening when she heard a footstep behind her. She came up fast, turning, ready to blast Lobo or Hawk for not trusting her.

But something hard smashed across the side of her head with shattering force before she had completely turned and the world exploded in a burst of fireworks . . .

★　★　★

Lobo exhaled smoke and stared at the half-smoked cigarette. 'Hawk — it's takin' her a long time.'

'Well, we dunno how complicated the hidey-hole is to get to — give her another couple of minutes.'

119

Lobo straightened, grimacing at a couple of knifing pains the movement caused him. 'No, she can't carry three bars of gold anyway. I'm goin' to look for her.'

Hawk sighed and followed Lobo out of the house and across the yard towards the barn with its one door swinging in the breeze.

They found the girl lying unconscious in front of the bin, oblong shapes in the spilled grain on the floor telling the story. The gold had been there: it wasn't now.

The narrow rear door was ajar and Lobo lunged towards it, palming up his six gun, as Hawk knelt beside the girl and examined the wound in her head which was bleeding slightly.

Lobo came hurrying back in less than a minute. 'Just glimpsed a rider goin' over the hogback. Looked like Dunbar.'

'Sonuver hit her pretty damn hard,' Hawk gritted. He raised one of her eyelids with his thumb and then the other. 'One pupil's bigger than the other — read somewhere that that ain't good. Hitch up the buckboard, Lobo. We better take her to a doctor.'

Lobo snapped his head up from checking the loads in his six gun. 'I'm goin' after Dunbar! He's got our gold!'

'Mebbe, mebbe not — but whether you go after him or not, get that buckboard hitched. I'll drive her into town to the sawbones.'

Lobo scowled, swung away, then said, 'Hell, you're in worse shape than me! You'd never make it. All right, I'll hitch up the buckboard and we'll all go into town. Dunbar won't make very good time weighed down with that gold. We'll catch up with him soon enough.'

Hawk stood stiffly and smiled. 'For a minute there thought I was gonna have to hold a gun on you.'

Lobo sobered, eyes narrowed. 'Don't ever do that, Hawk — I've had enough guns held on me these past few years. I'm liable to shoot first and ask questions afterwards I see a cocked gun pointed in my direction.'

He reached for some reins and traces on a post peg and lurched towards the rear door again.

Hawk watched him go: he knew the man meant what he said.

*   *   *

Dunbar almost made it.

The three bars of gold were heavy and straining in his work-worn saddle-bags and the left one, which contained two bars, had stretched the stitching so that the thread had popped and the seam had split open for a couple of inches.

His horse wasn't happy with the extra load, especially as it was unevenly distributed, but he spurred and whipped it over the hogback and then rode in a generally north-east direction that would take him past Rockslide Ridge. He could skirt Red Canyon where Mattie was holding her prime beef — separate from the untamed and unbranded brush-cows that Tallon and Purdy were rounding up. The prime beeves were hidden away from Harrigan whose men swung a wide loop on occasion. Only North's riders knew about the canyon.

Dunbar couldn't believe his luck, coming out of this with saddle-bags full of gold. Must be worth at least $1,000 a bar. Take him the best part of ten years to earn that even on top hand's pay. Anyway, the damn woman had more or less thrown in with that Lobo and Hawk, so that put her off-side with him. She had always been snooty, the way she bossed her men around.

And he would be glad to clear this country where he wouldn't have to worry about tangling with Lew Harrigan or Tip O'Malley every time he rode away from the ranch. No, he was headed for the bright lights now. Gonna whoop-'er-up, pleasure a slew of ladies, dose himself with redeye out of a sealed bottle instead of that puma piss they served across the bar, and push his luck to the limit with a few winning hands of cards. Yessir, he had a feeling his luck was changing for the better and he aimed to make the most of it.

He should never have let such a thought enter his head.

No sooner had he spoken out loud, riding in a wide swing past Rockslide Ridge, when his mount pricked up its ears and he heard the whinny of a horse. Dunbar swore, dropped a hand to his gun butt. *He didn't need any company right now! Aw, hell, it was probably Tallon or Purdy, they'd be up this way, hunting mavericks . . .*

He was so far wrong he just sat his horse and let his aching jaw sag as two riders came out of the brush.

Harrigan and Tip O'Malley.

He couldn't believe it. He'd just been thinking about them — and they had appeared, making straight for him.

Dunbar wheeled his mount and started to spur away, the horse grunting and snorting in protest at the weight of the gold on the left pulling hard. The hoofs scrabbled and stones flew and he lashed with the reins and his foul tongue but when the rifle shot whipped past his head he eased up the pressure on the horse and hauled rein.

Trouble was, he hauled too hard, throwing his weight back in the saddle, almost yanking the horse's forefeet clear of the ground. The saddlebags jarred and slewed and more stitching popped in the left one. He felt the blood drain from his face as a corner of one bar of gold protruded through the split about two inches.

Panicked, he snatched at his six gun and Tip O'Malley shot him out of the saddle with his rifle. Dunbar hit hard, the breath knocked out of him, and when he looked up Harrigan's horse was almost standing on top of him. Dunbar was bleeding from a wound high in the upper arm and it hurt like hell as he sat up, leery of the horse, holding one hand over the bullet hole.

'What's your hurry, Darkie?' Harrigan asked in a friendly tone. 'You gettin' uppity like that lady boss of yours, ain't even gonna pass the time of day?' He glanced across at O'Malley who was holding the smoking Henry on the downed man. 'Not a friendly type, is he, Tip?'

'Up to no good, is my guess, this close to our line,' O'Malley spat, watching Dunbar who fought to avoid looking at the saddle-bag with the corner of the gold bar showing. If only his horse would stay put.

'I — I just quit North,' he said, wincing as the pain started in his shoulder and arm. 'Fired me without backpay. Was lightin' a shuck an' din' feel like talkin'.'

'You never do,' Harrigan said. He tipped his hat to the back of his head, hooked a heel over the saddle-horn and reached into his shirt pocket for the makings. 'Mebbe I can stake you to a drink or two.'

Dunbar ran a tongue over his lips. *Don't move, you jughead!* his mind screamed as his horse pawed the ground restlessly. 'No, I — I got a little put away. I'll be right till I find another job.'

Harrigan paused in licking his cigarette paper, flicked his gaze to O'Malley. 'Well, well, well . . . '

'Now I wouldn't've believed it if I hadn't heard it with my own ears,' O'Malley said. 'A down-and-out cowpoke, just been fired without pay, refusin' the chance of a handout.'

Dunbar knew he had made a mistake but couldn't back down now. 'It's what I might have to do to earn the money.'

'Oh! You got a conscience now, Darkie? Hell, you been hidin' it well,' allowed Harrigan, finishing making his smoke and lighting up. He dropped the still-burning match on to Dunbar and the man writhed and swore, beating at the small flame, moaning with the pain of his wound.

His sudden movements spooked his horse and it whinnied, tossed its head, shied — and one of the gold bars thudded to the ground. Everything seemed to go still and silent. Dunbar actually heard the buzzing of bees and insects through the blood pounding in his head.

O'Malley was out of the saddle in a flash, picking up the bar easily in one big hand. He glanced up at Harrigan. 'It's just what it looks like, Lew . . . Confederate stuff.'

'It's mine!' bleated Dunbar, and those words brought the full attention of Harrigan and O'Malley on to him. 'I mean — Mattie gave it to me instead of backpay. I — I tried to throw you fellers off, I admit, but — '

He screamed and writhed and howled as O'Malley rammed his boot heel on to the bullet wound in his arm and screwed down hard, twisting, putting his weight behind it. Dunbar was actually sobbing by the time he eased up.

O'Malley leaned down closer. 'You a goddamn liar, Darkie. Try again. And this time you better tell your story straight.'

128

Dunbar did, with a lot of pauses to moan and grunt in pain, his arm limp at his side, the wound torn and bleeding profusely now. He told what he had heard outside the window and added quickly, 'They got a lot more stashed someplace — but I dunno where.'

Harrigan nodded gently and O'Malley rammed his boot once more into the now gaping wound. 'You sure?'

'I'm sure — I'm sure!' screamed Dunbar and Harrigan signed for O'Malley to ease up.

'You always were a loser, Darkie,' the rancher said.

'No, wait!' Sweat poured off Dunbar, blinding him. He wiped his eyes with a bloody hand, streaking his face. 'I — I can tell you where Mattie's got a prime herd of cows, not far from here. *Prime* beef, Lew! Not trash from the brush!'

'So? You tell us. And . . . ?'

Dunbar swallowed. 'You let me ride out.'

'With the gold, of course.'

'One bar! I ain't greedy — I keep one, you get the other two, one each. We got a deal?'

Harrigan arched his eyebrows and O'Malley said, 'Sounds OK to me, Lew.'

'Yeah — we get a gold bar and Mattie's prime herd. Where is it, Darkie?'

Dunbar hesitated. He knew what a risk he was taking revealing the hideout in Red Canyon: they could just kill him as soon as he told them. But what choice did he have? So he gave them deliberately vague directions to Red Canyon and Harrigan nodded. He had heard the place mentioned but hadn't known where it was, it being entirely on Mattie's land.

'So there really is a Red Canyon, huh? OK, Darkie, but you sure you'll be able to take your gold with you? That one bar, I mean?'

'Hell, yeah — I — I'll be all right once I get a bandage round my arm, Lew.'

'I dunno, Tip. I've always heard you can't take it with you.' Harrigan smirked but he saw that Dunbar hadn't detected his real meaning.

'Well, let's see.' O'Malley lifted his rifle and shot Dunbar through the chest.

Harrigan watched Dunbar fall, unmoving when he hit the ground, then: 'Ah, knew it was all hogwash. You *just can't* take it with you when you die. Look at that . . . all three bars still here.'

'Well, we can sure take it with us!' O'Malley grinned.

'Pick it up and we'll go find this Red Canyon — I can see how we can finish Mattie North and her damn full section right now!'

8

Wiped Out

Pagosa was a trading-post town. It had started out that way when the Indian reservation was operating and despite the extra houses and stores and two saloons, it was still little better than in the original trading post days.

It promised to grow into something decent, though, with folk moving in on the cheap land, encouraged by the Government that wanted Colorado Territory well-settled so it could be declared a State in the near future and thereby become eligible for Congress financial appropriations each year. It would also be wide open for those with strong political ambitions.

But it was still a town of straggling buildings and a winding, rutted main street when Lobo and Hawk drove in the buckboard with Mattie North in the back. She had regained consciousness briefly just after they had crossed the Durango River, but she did little more than say her head hurt before drifting away again.

Lobo hauled rein twice and asked the way to a doctor's from passers-by. The first men were trail drivers and didn't know where a doctor could be found. The second was a soldier who looked like he had travelled hard and far and he stared at them suspiciously, went to the side of the buckboard and peered in at the blanket-wrapped woman.

'What happened to her?' he demanded.

'Horse throwed her,' Hawk said. 'Hit her head.'

'Which is why we want to get her to a sawbones,' growled Lobo impatiently, earning a hard look from the soldier.

'Both you rannies look beat-up — been in a fight?'

'No, but could be we'll be in one in a minute if you don't tell us where to find the goddamn doctor!' Lobo was ready to back up his words and the soldier suddenly backed down, stepping away from the vehicle.

'One's got a shingle out in the second side street.' He pointed. 'Forge Lane — blacksmith's at the far end.'

Lobo nodded his thanks and flicked the reins, getting the buckboard moving. The soldier stood at the edge of the broken boardwalk and watched it go.

'Suspicious sonuver,' Hawk allowed, watching the soldier.

'Just throwin' his weight around.'

'We better take it easy if there's an army troop in town.'

'We'll leave the woman and get after Dunbar.'

'Best wait and see how she is — that was a hard crack she took. I can see bone in the bottom of the gash. It's not bleeding much but there's a helluva lot of bruising.'

The doctor showed concern over the wound, too, looked at her pupils and shook his head. 'Nasty concussion at least — brain might be bruised. You say she was thrown by a horse?'

He was a middle-aged man, none too clean-looking, but he seemed interested in the patient, wasn't in any hurry to throw them out.

'That's what we said, Doc,' Lobo told him soberly.

The man's mouth moved in a crooked smile. 'But not necessarily the truth.' He held up a hand quickly as Lobo startled to bristle. 'Friend, just relax — it's none of my business. She needs attention and that includes bed-rest. By rights I ought to report this to the captain of the army troop that's arrived in town, but I think we can get along very well without the Reconstruction rearing its ugly head around these parts. So, if you men have other business to take care of . . . ?'

'What about Mattie?' Hawk asked. 'How much will it cost?'

'Let me worry about that. Obviously you haven't worked for Mattie North for long or you'd know how highly she's regarded in this town. Instead of putting all her available money into prove up, as most homesteaders do, she gave over some to feed and clothe a big family who lost everything in a fire started by drunken cowpokes. She suspected one or two of her men were involved and felt responsible. None of the ranches where the rest of the cowboys worked contributed a red cent . . . so don't you worry about Mattie North. She'll be well taken care of.'

'Fine,' said Lobo. 'Let's go.'

But Hawk asked the doctor, 'When will she come round?'

'Can't tell — might be an hour or a week. But I think she'll probably be conscious by morning.'

'I'll look in then.'

Outside the ramshackle house as they walked towards the buckboard with their two mounts tethered to the tailgate, Lobo said, 'What the hell you stickin' around for? You heard the doc — she's in good hands. We gotta get on Dunbar's trail.'

'I'd like to make sure she's OK.'

Lobo stared at him strangely, then shrugged. 'OK — it's nearly dark anyway. We can bed down in the buckboard someplace, check with the doc come daylight, then go after Dunbar — that suit you?'

'Suits me fine,' Hawk said soberly, and Lobo picked up the reins of the buckboard as he climbed up into the seat, shaking his head slowly.

★ ★ ★

Harrigan and Tip brought three more men with them when they made their move on Red Canyon.

It was a rugged-looking place, spires and castellated forms weather-sculptured giving it an unreal appearance, backed by deep fissures in the sloping walls. It was surprisingly narrow-gutted, but there was a thin trickle of water from an underground spring wetting the floor of the canyon and then it widened into a small creek, nurturing a paddle-shaped area of grass.

This was where Mattie's herd was mostly, a few beasts having wandered down to where the water flowed over the rocks, making it cooler to drink. Two stood belly-deep in a dark pool and regarded the riders with only vague curiosity.

The rumble of the horses' hoofs echoed through the canyon — and woke Tallon and Purdy who had figured they had earned a rest after rounding up mavericks for most of the day. They had left the brush-bred cattle in a dead-end cutting, stacking lodgepoles across the open end. There was little feed and no water but they figured they would be OK overnight and they could drive them back for branding in the morning.

Then they had headed for Red Canyon where they could hobble their weary mounts on good grass and within a frog's leap of sweetwater. They knew of a snug cave there above where the herd was grazing and figured to have an early night, away from the eternal wind that moaned through the canyon.

Half-asleep, they stumbled to the cave entrance and in the fading light as sundown fire stained the sky high above, they saw the five riders splashing across the stream. They recognized Harrigan's crew right away.

'How the hell did he find this place!' demanded Tallon with a quaver in his voice for he knew they were in trouble.

'They're after the herd!' Purdy breathed as Tip O'Malley and a couple of the ranch hands started to ride around the cattle who were getting ready to bed down. 'Goddamnit!'

Tallon licked his lips, a six gun held down at his side now. 'Maybe they won't see us.'

'Our damn hosses are hobbled right under their noses!' snarled Purdy and even as he spoke Harrigan was sweeping his arm in an arc, obviously ordering a search for the horses' riders. 'We're in for a fight!'

He lunged for his warbag at the rear

of the cave and snatched up his rifle, a beat-up old Springfield with a modified Allin Trap Door breech system. It was single shot but tolerably accurate at fairly long ranges. He paused, looking at the ground, then grabbed a leather box of thick cartridges and hurried to the cave entrance, settling himself full-length behind a low rock. As he thumbed a cartridge into the breech he twisted his head to look at Tallon.

The man hadn't moved.

'Get over there, damn it! We're gonna have to fight whether you like it or not.'

Tallon looked at him, slowly shook his head. 'There's five of 'em.'

'So there's five and only two of us. What you want to do? Sit on your ass while they steal Mattie's herd?'

'They mightn't find us here.'

'Jesus! If you don't take the cake, you yellerbelly! Mattie's always treated us right.'

'It's how Harrigan and that O'Malley are gonna treat us that bothers me.'

'You took Mattie's money, now it's

time to earn it! You get your repeater and stretch out there or I'll put a bullet in you myself.'

'No! I don't wanna die!'

And before Purdy could stop him, Tallon ran out of the cave and started waving his arms, six gun holstered now, calling out.

'Hey! Hey! I don't wanna fight! You fellers do what you came for — I ain't gonna try an' stop you!'

He was running through the half dark, repeating his words, still waving his arms to show he wasn't holding a gun.

'It's the one called Tallon,' Tip O'Malley said, straining to see. He looked at Lew Harrigan. 'Likely Purdy's up there someplace with him.'

'Well, Tallon says he ain't gonna try and stop us — make sure he don't.'

O'Malley grinned, raised his rifle, sighted deliberately. Tallon saw him and skidded to a stop, almost falling.

'*Wait!* I ain't fightin'! I — '

'You sure ain't,' agreed O'Malley

quietly as he squeezed the trigger and Tallon was blown off his feet.

Hurt, floundering, he tried to stand and a second shot put him down for keeps.

'You not fightin' either, Purdy?' O'Malley called, looking up towards the dark cave entrance.

'The hell I'm not, you murderin' scum!'

The big Springfield's thunder filled the cave and almost deafened Purdy as he squeezed the trigger. O'Malley seemed to shake his head and then he was knocked out of the saddle, sprawling awkwardly as he hit the ground, rifle falling from his hands. He rolled quickly on to his belly, palming up his six gun, feeling the deep bullet burn across his left cheek with his other hand. Part of his ear lobe had also been clipped and blood was running down his neck, soaking his shirt collar. He swore and started shooting at the cave mouth an instant after Harrigan and the others raked the entrance with fire.

Purdy hunkered down, awkwardly loading another cartridge into his rifle breech as bullets whined and sang from his sheltering rock, chips flying. Some lead struck the sloping roof of the small cave and he was startled when a flattened bullet clipped the wooden stock of the Springfield, tearing it from his tingling fingers.

He snatched at it quickly and exposed part of his upper body as he did so. The guns hammered out there and he grunted and was flung back violently by lead slamming into his side. He managed to get the Springfield, lifted it across his body as a rider came thundering in for the finishing shot. Purdy triggered and the man's horse went down, somersaulting, dirt and stones rattling against Purdy's rock.

Then as the cowboy started to reload frantically, the L Bar H man staggered up the slope and crouched, triggering two fast shots. Purdy's small body jerked and was flung back and his hand opened involuntarily. The cartridge he was holding clattered to the cave floor as he flopped on to his face and was still, blood crawling out from beneath him.

'I got him!' the cowboy yelled, a rawboned ranny calling himself Waco. 'Dead as yest'y's bacon!'

'Just the two of 'em?' called Harrigan, watching as the dusty O'Malley stumbled towards him, holding a large kerchief against his face and neck.

'Looks like it,' Waco called.

'Goddamnit, make sure!'

'Yeah, no one else here, Lew.'

'All right,' Harrigan said. 'Get them cows rounded up. Waco, you and Kel and Jingles drive 'em to my south pasture — we'll change the brands tomorrow. Tip, you and me've got us a chore to do.'

O'Malley looked up, frowning. 'Tonight?'

'Tonight.' Then he saw the flash of Harrigan's teeth as he smiled. 'Always enjoy a fire more at night.'

★ ★ ★

The flames leapt fifteen feet high, with sounds like a volley of rifle fire.

The timber in the ranch house was not yet fully seasoned, still held sap in the pores and splinters, and this was what cracked and sputtered and hissed. Even the roar of the flames couldn't drown out the sounds. The window glass shattered metallically, one set of panes exploding outwards, whipping shards of glass through the night.

But Lew Harrigan and Tip O'Malley sat well back in the ranch yard on their nervous mounts, away from any danger. They had set a fire in the back of the barn, too, and this was just taking hold. They had released the few horses in the corrals and kicked over the chicken coop, the startled, awakened birds running around in wild circles, squawking.

'Make sure you pick up the horses tomorrow,' Harrigan said. 'Couple good mounts there.'

'Well, you sure wiped Mattie North off the map, Lew.' There was admiration in O'Malley's voice. He was still occasionally touching the bullet-burned cheek which was oozing a little blood now and then.

'Yeah, she won't be able to recover from this, and them two hardcases, Lobo and Hawk, won't have any reason for stayin'. I'll be able to make my move on that river land.' He stopped, frowning at the way O'Malley was looking at him. 'What . . . ?'

'Dunbar said she had more of that gold — maybe there's enough for her to make a comeback.'

Harrigan frowned more deeply. 'Ah, I think he was just talkin', hopin' we'd let him ride out, tryin' to get on our good side.'

He didn't sound convinced though.

'Dunbar might've been speakin' gospel, though.'

'Aw, damn you, Tip! I was feelin' mighty good a minute ago, now you've got my insides all knotted up again.'

O'Malley shrugged. 'Just pointin' out how it could be, Lew.'

Harrigan scrubbed a hand around his stubbled jaw and tugged at his moustache, nodding slowly. 'Possible, I s'spose. Anyway, we'll ride into Pagosa tomorrow and get these gold bars into the bank — '

'I'm exchangin' mine for cash.'

Harrigan looked steadily at O'Malley through the firelight. 'Tip — you work for me. You ain't my pardner.'

O'Malley smiled slowly. 'No — but I've earned me a bonus. That gold bar's mine, Lew — you've already got two to my one, but you want to argue about it and we'll settle things right now.'

He dropped a hand to his gunbutt.

Harrigan fumed but he felt the lurch in his belly, too. He knew he wouldn't stand a chance against a killer like Tip O'Malley in a fast-draw square-off.

He smiled tightly. 'You're right. You have earned it. Well, there goes the roof of the house cavin' in, and the barn's well alight now. We might's well head back home and grab some shut-eye. What I call a good night's work.'

9

Desperate

They had taken the buckboard into the trees behind the doctor's house, hobbled the team and their mounts, and turned in on their bedrolls spread in the back of the vehicle.

It was so hard sleeping on the rough boards that sometime during the night, feeling only half-awake, Hawk took his bedroll and spread it on the grass. He was moving stiffly for his aches and pains seemed to have intensified since the ride in from the North ranch, but he had a better sleep and awoke as the first rays of sunlight spilled over the hogback rise behind the town.

He thought it was his senses that had awakened him so early. He was eager to make sure the girl was all right, but as he sat up on his blankets and squeezed some of the sleep out of his face he heard the sounds of someone pounding on the doctor's front door.

Lobo must have heard, too, for he poked his head over the edge of the buckboard, blinking.

'Somethin' up?'

'Could be — it is a sawbones' house.'

'Better check.'

Hawk was already standing, groping for his hat and then his boots and gunbelt. Lobo already had his hat jammed on his head, quickly tugged on his boots and grabbed his gunbelt as he clambered down from the buckboard.

They could hear voices on the doctor's front porch now and hurried around the side of the house. Someone was just leaving through the front gate and Hawk recognized him as Monk Taylor, one of Mattie's neighbours.

'Been an accident, Monk?' Hawk called and the man spun around, came back into the yard, looking worried.

He was a family man working hard to prove up on his quarter-section slightly to the north of Mattie's place and looked a lot older than his thirty-eight years.

'No accident, Hawk — it was deliberate.'

'What was?' Hawk felt a coldness in his belly.

'Mattie's house and barn burned down last night. I — I ain't sure and I'll deny I said it if ever you ask me in front of witnesses, but I reckon it was Lew Harrigan and Tip O'Malley.'

'You see 'em do it?' snapped Lobo and Monk shook his head.

'Seen 'em ridin' towards Mattie's place, though, and when O'Malley tossed a loop over the corral poles and set the remuda a'runnin', I hurried on home and got the wife and kids battened down in the storm cellar. I figured if Harrigan was on the rampage . . . ' His words trailed off and he shrugged awkwardly.

'Obliged, Monk. How'd you know Mattie was here?'

'Was in town, seen you drive in, was

gonna come see what was wrong but that soldier you spoke to started throwin' his weight around, clearin' the side-walks of us loungers. Was when I was ridin' home I spotted Harrigan.'

'Thanks again, Monk. Don't worry about Harrigan. He won't bother you.'

'He always bothers me, just by breathin',' Monk Taylor said and went back out the gate towards his lathered horse tied to the picket fence.

Inside, they found that the doctor had already told Mattie the news.

She looked a lot better than when Hawk had last seen her, a bandage around her head. But she was still very pale, her face drawn, mouth tight, all no doubt a reaction to the bad news.

'You should've left it, Doc,' Hawk said harshly.

'Fully intended to but she heard Monk — he was plenty excited and talking loud.' The doctor started fussing, taking her pulse and feeling her forehead but she was in no mood for his attentions.

She looked past his shoulder at Lobo and Hawk. 'I'm ruined!' she said softly, her voice very shaky.

'Maybe Monk was mistaken,' Hawk began, but one hard look from Mattie and he broke off, nodded jerkily. 'Yeah, sounds like Harrigan. Playing mighty rough.'

'Kicking someone when they're down,' Mattie corrected him. 'It's his style — he saw his chance to wipe me out and he took it! Oh, *damn* him! *Damn* him!'

She tried to hold back the tears but couldn't manage it. The doctor became concerned at first, but then decided perhaps it would be best for her to get rid of her frustrations and hurt this way.

'Perhaps you men ought to go have breakfast or something.'

'No!' Mattie jerked her head up, dabbing at her eyes, frowning. 'Oh, this blamed headache! Hawk — Lobo — I'm finished now. It was Dunbar who hit me and presumably stole the gold bars. I have very little money left in the bank. I can't pay you but — would you stay and help me?'

They exchanged glances but she couldn't read anything into it. Neither spoke for a short time.

'We figured to go after Dunbar,' Lobo said.

'If we catch up with him, we'll get the gold back,' Hawk added, grim-faced.

'Yes — I guess you will. But the last I heard, you were claiming that gold as yours.'

'Not quite,' Hawk corrected her. 'There were three bars and we aimed to split, remember — one bar each for you, Lobo and me.'

It was her turn to be silent. Then, 'Well, I — I didn't really think — I'm sorry. I didn't have very much trust in you.'

Hawk frowned. 'I give my word, lady, I stand by it.'

Lobo said nothing, kept his face blank.

'I'm sorry,' she said again, irritably wiping away a stray tear. She started to throw the blankets aside but the doctor stopped her, shaking his head emphatically.

'No you don't, young woman — you're staying right there in bed for at least three days.'

'I am not!'

'You are! It's utterly ridiculous for you to even contemplate getting up. Here! Try and walk across the room — go on. Someone will catch you when you fall.'

Defiantly, she swung her legs over the side of the bed and immediately fell back on to the pillows, grabbing wildly at the sheets, fisting them up tightly as her eyes rolled in her head and she gasped, 'Everything's — spinning.'

The doctor merely smiled patiently and helped her to a sitting position again, rearranging the pillows for her comfort, drawing the bedclothes up.

'Do you wish to review your decision to leave, Mattie?' he asked quietly and she merely stared, gave a sigh and nodded gently.

'Will you — help me?' she asked Lobo and Hawk.

Hawk nodded. 'We have scores to settle with Harrigan and O'Malley, too.'

'You do, anyway,' Lobo said quietly and fell silent at the look Hawk threw in his direction.

'We'll see if we can catch up with Dunbar,' Hawk told her.

'I'd say, professionally speaking, that you could do with some bed-rest, too, Hawk,' the doctor said.

'I'll be OK, Doc. Rest easy, Mattie. We'll get the gold back.'

Her face fell. 'Yes, I believe that. But I — I'm afraid it may be already too late for it to do me much good . . . '

★ ★ ★

Because Lobo had seen Dunbar riding over the hogback, they started out towards the trail that he would have taken from that point if — as they were sure he would — he was aiming to leave this neck of the woods.

Hawk was riding stiffly and going slow enough to make Lobo curse with impatience.

'I'm gonna ride on ahead an' try to pick up his trail,' he said, already spurring his horse away. 'I'll signal when I find it.'

'Don't alarm him if he's still close!' Hawk called but he knew it was unnecessary: Lobo wouldn't blow this chore. He was too eager to get his hands on that gold.

He signalled from a ledge over towards Rockslide that he had picked up Dunbar's trail, but as he turned away and dropped out of sight quickly, Hawk knew he wouldn't be waiting around. By now Hawk had developed a kind of numbness in the saddle, his body fighting back against the constant movement and its effect on his stiff joints.

But he touched his spurs to the black's flanks and gritted his teeth as it broke into a run. He made pretty good time to the area of the ledge and when he skirted the rise and saw the long scar of Rockslide he was surprised to see Lobo squatting down in the shade of a tree, smoking, his mount standing by with trailing reins.

'Lose the trail?' he asked as he drew closer and Lobo looked up slowly, shook his head, pointing off to one side and slightly behind him.

Hawk reined in, craned his neck. He saw disturbances on the ground, a dark patch, and what looked like drag marks leading into the brush and timber.

'Is that dark patch blood?'

'Yep — and Dunbar's. He's back in there a few yards. Dead now, but he was still alive when I found him.'

Lobo stared at him steadily and Hawk had the feeling that the man was kind of challenging him. He dismounted with a grunt, eased the kinks out of his hips and knees, walked stiffly over to the place Lobo indicated.

Dunbar lay on his back. He had been shot twice, looked like — once in the upper arm, once in the chest. The latter was probably fatal but Hawk wasn't sure. There were other marks on the man — recent marks of violence.

Lobo ambled up and Hawk looked at him bleakly. 'He say anything before he died?'

'Couple of things.'

'He — volunteer them?'

Lobo shrugged. 'I had to kinda persuade him a little. All he wanted to do was die.'

'You seem to be pretty good at helping fellers like that get where they want to go.' Lobo said nothing, didn't avert his gaze. Hawk saw there was a challenge there but he didn't feel up to taking him up on it right now. 'What were his last words?'

'Couldn't make 'em out — but managed to pick up a few things. Important one is that Harrigan's got the gold. Him and Tip O'Malley. And somethin' about Red Canyon.'

'That's where Mattie keeps her best herd — she told me about it but I haven't been there yet.'

'Me neither, but reckon I can find it. You hear what I said? Harrigan's got the gold.'

'I heard. We know where it is then, don't we? But we don't know what's happened to Mattie's herd.'

'Not really our concern is it?' Lobo spoke slowly and firmly. 'The gold is what we're after.'

'We said we'd help Mattie, too.'

'You did.'

Hawk narrowed his eyes. 'Thought I was speaking for both of us.'

Lobo sighed. 'Look, Hawk, I been chasin' this gold for nigh on four years. I had it within reach and it was took from me. Now I know where it is again — and I want it. Like I want the rest of it that Denny Brackett said was buried somewhere up here.'

Hawk looked around. 'Up where? This is a damn big country, Lobo. Sure, I'd be happy to get my hands on a bar or two of the gold, but we can't let Mattie down.'

'We don't owe her nothin'.'

'Mebbe you don't.'

Lobo shook his head in slow exasperation. 'I blamed well knew it! I knew way back at Kettledrum — I seen it in you when I first mentioned findin' the papers about the transfer to the bank of the gold. Sure, you were eager enough, but there was just — *somethin'* — there that gave me a twitch in the gullet and I said to myself, 'Myron, this Reb is good, thinks fast, fights like ten Injuns, but there's somethin' in him that's gonna flare up one of these days and you're gonna have trouble with him.' He paused and spat. 'Goddamnit — I was right!'

'You heard me tell Mattie. I give my word, I stand by it.'

'I heard, but she was plannin' on keepin' the gold for herself, didn't aim to share with us till she got real desperate and there weren't no other way out for her. I said right from the very beginnin' and I say it again now, it's *finders keepers!* Now that's the way I look at it and if you ain't gonna go along with it — well.' He scratched at one ear. 'Could be you and me are at the partin' of the ways.'

He used his left hand to scratch his ear and when he was sure he had Hawk's attention, his right swept up the six gun out of his holster, the hammer cocking.

'Sorry, Hawk — really am. But three bars are better'n one.'

Hawk had stiffened and his eyes were pinched way down now. He stared at Lobo unflinchingly in a long silence.

'Lobo,' he said very quietly, 'you once told me never to point a cocked pistol at you or you'd ram it down my throat. I feel the same way about having one pointed at me.'

'Yeah, I know, and I didn't want to do it, but I don't see any choice.'

'There's always a choice — but you'll never tackle Lew Harrigan and O'Malley alone. They won't take time to talk. They spot you, they'll kill you.'

Lobo smiled crookedly. 'I spot them

first — which I aim to do — I'll kill *them*.'

Hawk nodded. 'Might work. If they're carrying the gold. What if they've already hidden it?'

'Ah, the hell with 'what ifs'. I'm doin' it my way like I should've all along. Really sorry, Hawk. I like you — we could get along together. But you need to get rid of some of them soft spots. Too damn full of Southern pride.'

Hawk spread his hands. 'Where do we go from here?'

'Guess I'm gonna have to tie you up and — '

That was as far as he got. Hawk was standing on ground slightly up-slope and when he kicked out his boot was on a level with Lobo's gunhand. The toe of the boot drove into the back of Lobo's hand and jarred it painfully against the butt of the six-shooter. Lobo grunted in pain and the gun fell and then Hawk stepped in close, slugged him on the jaw, drove two solid blows into his midriff and, when Lobo doubled over, clubbed him on the back of the neck.

Lobo sprawled, face scraping on the gravel as he slid a couple of feet down the slope. Hawk stepped after him and Lobo swept out an arm and yanked his legs from under him. Hawk fell, twisting in towards the man, driving his knees into Lobo's chest. The man grunted as breath gusted out of him and he tried to throw a punch into Hawk's groin.

Hawk wrenched a hip around in time, drove a right hook that glanced off the other's head. Lobo rolled away, kicking, his boots knocking Hawk full length. Hawk spun on his buttocks as Lobo launched himself at him, face contorted and bloody, hands clawed, ready to choke the life out of his adversary. Hawk ducked his head, putting his chin deep against his upper chest and lifted his knees. Lobo gagged as they took him in the belly, his full weight adding to the effectiveness of the manoeuvre.

He rolled off, grasping his middle,

desperate for breath. Hawk lunged across, crushed his face in one big hand and slammed his head against a deadfall. Lobo slumped and Hawk fell away, gasping, holding a hand against his bleeding nose.

After a while, when he could breathe again more or less normally, he took Lobo's lariat from the man's saddle and tied him up hand and foot in such a way that the man could work his way free in a couple of hours. He placed the six gun and Lobo's rifle high up in the branches of a tree simply by weighting the remainder of the lariat with a stone, tossing it over a high branch, then tying the guns on. He hauled them up and threw the loose coils of rope as high as he could up amongst the branches. They caught and though the guns slipped down a couple of feet, Lobo would be kept mighty busy trying to retrieve them.

'You better pray we never meet again.' Lobo's words were slurred but menacing as he came round, already fighting his bonds.

'When you get free, go get your gold, Lobo. Don't come looking for me or you'll never live long enough to enjoy it.'

Then Hawk mounted his black and rode out, trying to remember what he had heard about the location of Red Canyon.

10

'That Damn Gold!'

There were two cows drinking at the stream when Hawk finally located Red Canyon and found a way in.

They looked up at the sound of his horse and went back to drinking, unworried by his presence. There were no more animals in evidence but the churned-up ground told him the story of how the main herd had been driven out. These two at the stream must have somehow escaped the rustlers' notice. He looked around him as he rolled a smoke. When he was lighting up he saw the dark maw of the cave and then a bundle of rags that he knew wasn't that at all. He ground out the vesta underfoot, held the cigarette between his lips and hurried up the slope.

He found Purdy first. The man had

bled a lot but was still breathing and had a faint pulse. He ran to the other body and saw that Tallon was beyond help. There wasn't a lot he could do for Purdy. The wound had stopped bleeding now and he didn't want to wash away the congealed blood in case it started up again, so he tore up Tallon's shirt and made a crude bandage, caught Purdy's mount and brought it over beside a rock. It took him some time but he eventually managed to get Purdy roped into the saddle.

He heaved Tallon's body over the man's horse and roped his wrists to his ankles under the animal's belly. By then Hawk was about exhausted and he reckoned he had aches and pains over his aches and pains, but he rode out of that canyon slowly, with his cocked rifle resting across his thighs, leading the two horses.

It was a long ride back to Pagosa, but Purdy would die if he didn't get him to a sawbones. At least he had to try.

It would be another hard blow for

Mattie North, too, her cowhands dead and her prime herd rustled.

There was no law in Pagosa but the army was visiting. Maybe they could do something to help her.

If not, it would be up to him.

Trouble was, he wasn't sure if he was up to doing the job.

* * *

Lew Harrigan and Tip O'Malley were waiting on the porch for the bank doors to open.

Harrigan was quieter than usual and O'Malley caught him a couple of times looking sidelong at him, hard-eyed, jaw knotted. It didn't worry the big ranny. He knew Harrigan was sour because he hadn't managed to bully Tip out of that bar of gold. The man was greedy to the point of obsession.

Hell, most of the trouble on the range was simply because of Harrigan's greed. He didn't really need that river access land the girl had claimed from the Lands Agency. It would make things easier, but he already had some access to the river and it was simply that she had officially filed on it in her name when he'd aimed to use it, as and if he needed to — without official registration and so without the need to prove up.

He had aimed to bully anyone else who might have notions of moving in for there was no real law hereabouts. Army visits were infrequent and they weren't much interested in homesteaders' feuds, anyway. No, he wanted that land simply because he *didn't* want anyone else to have it, sure not Mattie North.

Not that it mattered now. He had ruined her overnight and she would have to clear out because there was no way she could prove up on the extra three sections she had filed on. Harrigan was snake-smart and snake-mean, too.

The doors opened and Harrigan nodded to the somewhat startled bank clerk and pushed by, carrying his saddle-bags with the gold bars. O'Malley followed, his lone bar wrapped in an old sack.

A stern-faced woman in a drab grey frock and with her hair pulled back severely, tried to stop them from going through the low gate that led to the clerks' area, beyond which was the door to the banker's office.

'You'll have to wait!' she snapped. 'Banker never sees anyone during the first half-hour. If you'll be good enough to come back then — '

'If he's in, he'll see us,' Harrigan said and pushed past rudely.

O'Malley grinned at her and slapped her buttock, bringing a shocked cry from the woman. Her face coloured and her eyes widened and then they filled with tears, and she thrust a small lace handkerchief against her gasping mouth, turned and hurried through a door leading into the non-public part of the bank.

Banker Spence was annoyed when

Harrigan slapped open the office door and, followed by Tip O'Malley, strode across the room and dumped his two gold bars on the banker's desk. Tip added his and Spence frowned down at them for a long minute before raising his eyes to the two men.

'How much?' Harrigan asked.

'I'll have to have the gold assayed for purity and — *this is Confederate gold!*' He looked startled, eyes swivelling from one man to the other.

'It's gold — and it's stamped twenty-two carat,' Harrigan pointed out. 'That's all you need to know. All we need to know is how much you're offering.'

Banker Spence sat back in his chair, knowing that he had the upper hand here as usual. Anyone sitting or standing across the desk from him wanted the bank's money and that made him a powerful man due respect — and he would have it!

'I am required by Reconstruction Law to report any Confederate gold that comes to light — so, I'm sorry, gentlemen. Captain Garrett and his troop are in town right now and it's my bounden duty to report this gold to him. You'll have forms to fill out and there will be a wait while it's decided just what will happen to the gold — depending on its origins, I should think, and . . . '

Harrigan leaned closer across the desk and Spence started, thrusting back in his chair, blood starting to drain from his face when he saw the man's hard eyes.

'Banker, you live in a fine house, finest in town, unless I miss my guess. Got a nice family, too, I hear, couple daughters and a baby son. Now, if some night that house of yours somehow caught fire, all those nice folk would be in danger. And so would you — but it's not likely to happen, I guess. Just pointin' out to you what *could* happen and all the rules and regulations you live by wouldn't be worth a damn hill of beans, would they?'

'You — you're threatening me!' Spence gasped, sweating.

Harrigan looked shocked, turned towards O'Malley.

'Tip, did you hear me threaten the banker?'

'Not me, Lew — like you said, you were just pointin' out some of the dangers of livin' in this town where there ain't any law ninety per cent of the time . . . '

'That's right. You savvy what I'm sayin', banker? This Captain Garret and his men'll move on to the next town and who knows when we'll see them again? He don't hear about this gold before he moves out, you'd just have to wait to report it to him next time around. You could do that, couldn't you? If you forget, hell, who'd blame you?'

Spence wiped sweat from his face and O'Malley picked up a tintype in a silver frame from the desk, looking at the smiling woman, two young girls in pigtails and a babe in arms.

'Nice family, banker. House looks real good in the background, too.'

'This — this is outrageous!'

Harrigan lost patience, slapped a hand on the desk.

'How much for the gold bars, banker? You better make a guess — and a damn *good* guess — or I'll stay here while Tip rides out to take a look at that house of yours. Family in or out this mornin' . . . ?'

Spence slumped. 'I — I won't forget this, Harrigan!'

Lew Harrigan thrust a finger into the man's face. 'Now that's a right good idea, banker — don't you *never* forget what I said. OK, make us an offer.'

★   ★   ★

The doctor straightened and pressed his hands into the small of his back, sighing briefly.

He looked down at the pale, unshaven face of Purdy, his features stark against the clean sheet that was drawn up to his chin and then turned to Hawk.

'I'll be surprised if he makes it. He's lost a deal of blood and must have an iron constitution to have lived so long with that bullet in his chest. It's done a lot of damage inside.'

Hawk nodded. 'He say anything?'

The doctor frowned. 'Just one word — I'm not sure what it was.' He paused, looking closely at Hawk. 'If I had to guess, I'd say — 'Harry'.'

Hawk smiled faintly. 'Or the first part of 'Harrigan'.'

'That's possible. Unless Tallon's first name was Harry. He and Purdy were friends, weren't they?'

'Just bunk mates. You know my guess is the right one, Doc.'

'Well, if you want to believe that it's up to you.'

'Do what you can for him, Doc,' Hawk said and left the room, going down to the one where Mattie North was.

She was propped up on pillows in the

bed with her eyes closed.

'Asleep?' he asked quietly as he entered, and she opened her eyes and shook her head gently.

'Just resting my eyes — my vision is still strange. Blurred, double at times. How's Purdy?'

'Not too good. Seems it was Harrigan, which we more or less figured anyway. He's burned you out, taken the gold, and stolen your herd.'

She nodded very gently. 'I — I've been thinking about it. The quarter-section I've already proved up on is mine, but I don't have the money to rebuild, so I suppose Harrigan can walk in on all or part of what was once my land and I won't be able to do anything about it.'

'You can stop him moving in in the first place.'

Her eyes seemed to have trouble focusing on him. 'How?'

'I'll do it.'

After a pause she asked, 'Why?'

He shrugged. 'Said I'd help you and

177

right now it seems I'm all you got.'

'I wasn't going to share that gold with you and Lobo, you know. Not if I could help it. I — I was too desperate.'

'I know. It's always been a kind of dream thing, that gold, to me. Just out of reach whenever I came close to touching it. I've never really depended on it — not like Lobo. He was obsessed with it.'

'You're a strange man, Hawk — and you haven't told me where Lobo is.'

'He's going after his gold.'

'It's not his! I found it!'

There was a brightness flaring in her eyes now and he said, 'That damn gold! It's always been a trouble. Harrigan's likely cashed it in by now anyway, so none of you'll get your hands on it again.'

'You sound almost — happy at the thought!'

'Told you, it never seemed real to me.'

'No — '

He thought she was going to say

more, ask him to go after Harrigan, but she merely shrugged.

'There's nothing to be done, I suppose.'

'Told you, there's me — I owe Harrigan and O'Malley. Don't think I'll get your gold back, but I'll do what I can to keep him from grabbing your land.'

'I — I want you to do it, but I can't let you go it alone. You wouldn't stand a chance.'

'I work best alone. Lobo and me, we made a good team, but we see things different where the gold's concerned.' She suddenly stiffened. 'You said he'd gone after the gold. Does that mean you — you'll be up against Lobo as well?'

'Looks that way.'

'Oh, Hawk, everything's such a mess!' Suddenly, she looked up sharply. 'Wait! You and Lobo told me there's more gold yet! The rest of the two hundred thousand!'

'No one knows where it is, for sure.

Brackett figured it was buried not all that far from where you found the stash on Rockslide Ledge, but if Lobo learned any more details he didn't tell me.'

Disappointment showed plainly on her face. Then she brightened. 'Purdy! Some time back now he reported he had seen a couple of strange riders crossing North land, not far from the Red Canyon trail. Their legs were caked with red mud and he back-trailed them. That was when he found Red Canyon was suitable for holding cattle. Up till that time we thought it was a dead end just a few yards in from the entrance . . . it's possible those riders might have been in there burying the gold!'

'You're drawing a long bow, Mattie. I have to be moving if I'm going to do anything at all.'

'Well just what are you going to do, Hawk?'

'Play it by ear. Don't worry, Mattie. Things'll work out.'

She seemed unconvinced — or was it

only that her mind was elsewhere. Like Red Canyon?

★ ★ ★

Hawk was tired and although the stiffness was slowly leaving his battered body, he felt more like resting than riding out looking for tracks. He decided he could use a drink and turned into the biggest saloon-cum-whorehouse in town. It was called The Hot Spot.

It was crowded, a lot of soldiers mingling with the cowhands and freighters and dancehall girls. There seemed to be a continuous stream of weary-eyed painted women leading staggering men up the stairs to the private rooms on the upper floor. They passed other couples coming down, usually with the man's clothing still in disarray.

Hawk stood just inside the batwings looking round the room, holding his Henry rifle down at his side. He preferred the long gun to his Remington pistol, simply because the rifle held sixteen rimfire cartridges, whereas the six gun had to be loaded with powder and lead and percussion caps, chamber by chamber in the cylinder. If there was going to be trouble, the brass-actioned Henry was his weapon of choice.

He stiffened, just moving his gaze away from the stairs, then swung it back swiftly. Tip O'Malley was coming down with a heavy, plodding tread, one arm about the ample waist of one of the whores. She had a false smile pasted on her face, looked tired and disinterested, but allowed him to fondle one of her breasts as they descended.

At the foot of the stairs she pushed O'Malley away and he slapped her, snarled something, and literally beat his way to the bar. Hawk started forward and heard Tip's rough voice calling to the 'keep.

'Gimme a bottle of that rotgut, barman! A whole bottle! No — not the rotgut. Make it one of them bonded ones with the fancy labels — *Red Bird*. Yeah — that one. Sure I can pay, got plenty.'

Hawk came up behind O'Malley as the barkeep placed the bottle of whiskey, in a wrapping of tissue paper, on the counter, not relinquishing his grip on the neck until O'Malley pushed a pile of silver coins across.

O'Malley put away the remainder of his money and was just reaching for the whiskey when Hawk swung the rifle and the barrel shattered the bottle, splashing its contents all over Tip's shirt and arms and face, the liquid dribbling off the bar top.

There was a lot of jostling as men hurriedly moved out of the way and Tip O'Malley was left standing alone at the bar, dripping. He turned quickly, eyes blazing, widening in disbelief as he recognized Hawk.

'You son of a *bitch*!'

He snatched the neck of the broken bottle and lunged at Hawk who stepped to one side, clipping O'Malley across the head with the flat of the rifle stock. Tip staggered, dropping the bottle, clawed at the bar edge, one leg buckling. Hawk stepped in and slammed the rifle against that leg and O'Malley fell further, hit his face against the lead edging, hat falling off. Hawk grabbed O'Malley's lank hair and smashed his forehead into the edge again.

Tip went down to hands and knees, shaking his head, blood dripping. Hawk kicked him solidly in the ribs, driving the big body against the bar. Tip started to slide down and Hawk lifted first one knee, then the other, into the man's face. The big cowhand's head cracked against the woodwork and he toppled sideways, mouth slack, blood on his chin, his nose hammered to one side.

Hawk went down on one knee, groped in the barely-conscious man's pockets and took his money. He straightened, rifle at the ready, under the hard stare of the crowd.

'He stole something from me and

sold it. This is what's left of what he got for it.'

'We only got your word for that,' said a corporal with a heavy moustache.

The Henry's barrel swung up an inch or two. 'You do. You got anything against taking the word of a Southerner?'

The corporal swallowed. 'If I did, I ain't now.'

Hawk smiled faintly. He nudged the moaning O'Malley. Then, still holding the rifle with his thumb on the hammer spur, he backed to the side door and went outside and made his way back to Main.

He turned towards the doctor's house in Forge Lane, watched by a couple of soldiers over the top of the saloon's batwings.

11

Shoot-Out!

'There's just over seven hundred dollars there,' Hawk told the astonished girl as he handed her all the money he had taken from O'Malley.

But — how — ?'

'He was living it up so I knew he must've cashed in his share of the gold bars. Likely only one. It's yours. Get you started on rebuilding.'

She shook her head very slowly as she watched his face. 'You — you're an amazing man, Hawk. What *is* your real name, anyway?'

'Chris Winters, but Hawk suits me better somehow.'

'You're still amazing. You knew I planned on keeping that gold if I could and yet you did . . . this.'

'I don't think you would've.

You'd've shared.'

She coloured a little. 'You can't know that — I feel ashamed for even thinking about not sharing. Anyway, I'm very grateful, but surely O'Malley will come after you.'

'Reckon so. But that's OK — we're due a square-off.'

'It doesn't bother you? To go up against a man like that?'

'He's mean and he's got a killer streak, but I've faced down worse. Anyway, it's inevitable so no use a'worrying about it. It's gonna happen — just a matter of when.'

He stood and put on his hat.

'I'll be going now. Don't know when I'll be back, but I will be, some time.'

'Don't go too far, Hawk,' she said quietly. 'I — I wouldn't care to think you were so far away I would never see you again.' She was blushing once more.

'Told you — I'll be back.' He smiled. 'Doc say's you can start walking around tomorrow if your eyes are OK.'

'Yes, they've settled down a bit now. Good luck, Hawk. For whatever you have planned.'

He nodded and left, passing the infirmary section where the doctor was working over Purdy. The medic looked up and signed to Hawk that he wanted a word with him. They met at the infirmary door.

'Purdy's rallying. Just a little. Wanted to know how he got here of course — he wants to see you.'

Hawk frowned slightly. 'In kind of a hurry, Doc — '

'I think it might be to your advantage to have a word with him.'

Hawk shrugged and moved to Purdy's bedside. In Hawk's opinion, the cowboy looked worse than when he had brought him in, but he opened his eyes and focused on Hawk.

'Obliged, Hawk,' he said in a hoarse whisper. 'Listen — back o' that cave — '

'Yeah, saw your bedroll and warbag but I left 'em there. You can go back for 'em when you get well.'

Purdy was already shaking his head before Hawk finished speaking. 'Forget 'em. First time I've ever used the cave, though Tallon an' me knew it was there. Signs in the back somethin' mighta been buried there. Small — mounds — '

He was gasping by now, fighting to get out the words. Hawk placed a hand on his good shoulder.

'Easy — I'll take a look if I can. You better rest, *amigo*.'

Purdy's eyes were wide as he stared hard at Hawk and his mouth worked but no intelligible sounds came. Hawk nodded and stood, walked back to the door where the doctor waited.

'He might seem better but he don't look it.'

'He's been saving his energy to tell you something.'

Hawk glanced back at Purdy, tossed him a casual salute. 'Yeah — well, take care of him, Doc. He seems a pretty good man.'

189

'Getting scarcer by the day in this town.'

Hawk smiled and left by the side door where he had tied his black to the hitching ring built into the side of the old house. He had his left boot in the stirrup and was starting to swing up his other leg when the rifle cracked from the trees and simultaneously a bullet caromed off his saddlehorn.

Hawk threw himself back, grabbing at his rifle.

As he hit the ground, the hidden gun fired twice more and bullets kicked dirt against his rolling body, under the legs of the horse. It stomped and tossed its head and Hawk whipped off his hat and slapped it hard in the belly, growling, 'Get outta here!'

The horse needed no second bidding as a fourth slug seared its arched neck. It whinnied, reared and lunged away. By then Hawk was in against the side of the house, working the lever of the Henry as he slewed around on his belly.

The gunsmoke pinpointed the bush-whacker pretty good although it was dissipating quickly in the breeze. He pumped three fast, raking shots into the shadowed trees, bracketing the place where he figured the smoke originated. Leaves erupted with small twigs and then a whole bush seemed to move violently before going still again.

He slammed two more shots into this, low down, and it jerked again. But the rifle over there also triggered and splinters flew from the clapboards above him in a long, gouging line and he ducked his head and upper body.

The killer sent two more shots in Hawk's direction and then he heard the sounds of bushes being moved violently as someone lurched through. Hawk rolled on to his side, squinted, saw the movement under the trees and rose to one knee, triggering fast.

No gun answered him this time.

He hunched up, snatching his hat and jamming it on his head as ran forward, zigzagging, crouched almost double. He paused when he was closer, fired ahead of where he saw the leaves swaying and jerking. There was a crash and, as he sprinted forward, the killer's gun crashed twice. A slug cut air past his face causing him to twist involuntarily. He fell, rolling, losing the rifle briefly and by the time he had snatched it up again and smashed his way into the brush, he heard hoofbeats going away from him.

He slammed and kicked and cussed his way through the clinging brush and when he reached a point where he could see over it and beyond into sparser timber, he was just in time to see a horseman going over the rise.

He'd have bet his left eyeball that it was Tip O'Malley.

Which came as no surprise, really, but Hawk swore again when he saw that his mount had run clear across the doctor's yard and jumped the rear fence and was somewhere back in the heavier timber, no doubt resting and awaiting collection by its angry owner.

By the time he got mounted, O'Malley would be lost in the foothills. But Hawk wanted this finished now: he had enough on his mind without worrying about when O'Malley was going to bushwhack him again and try to settle their score.

The horse was in a devilish mood — *when the hell weren't they when you needed 'em most?* he thought bitterly — and he was still moving stiffly so it took him some time before he caught the animal. He heard and glimpsed folk back at the doctor's, attracted by the shooting, gathered to see what it was all about. There were a couple of army uniforms there so Hawk kept the timber between him and them and rode away fast.

There had been blood on the ground and on some of the leaves of the bushes where O'Malley had pushed through, so he knew the man was wounded. How badly was anybody's guess at this time, but the occasional splash of bright blood gave him a direction and he picked up Tip's trail.

The man was heading in the general direction of L Bar H as he would have reckoned so he didn't try to follow the trail directly, but cut across the hills, figuring to catch up with his quarry near the Red Canyon country, or, at least, to have closed the gap by that time.

Then, off to his left, he heard the crash of gunfire, the ragged volley of a shoot-out, drifting through the hills.

Hawk hesitated, frowning. It could be that Tip O'Malley had reached about the point where he figured the gunfire to be coming from. But who the hell would he be fighting in his present shape . . . ? Well, he didn't know just what shape Tip was in. It was all guesswork . . .

'Ah, to hell with it!' he snapped aloud, wrenching on the reins and spurring the horse forward.

He knew he was going over there to check on what was happening. Why delay?

As he rode, he fumbled out fresh rimfire cartridges and thumbed them home into the Henry's tubular magazine.

★ ★ ★

Hawk was leery, figuring it could be a trap, although he was sure there had been at least two different guns, one making a flatter sound than the other.

So he rode in warily — but even so, they almost got him.

He was just about convinced that O'Malley himself had done the shooting, using his six gun and his rifle for the sounds of different guns, inferring there was more than one man involved. Hopefully, this would make Hawk think that Tip himself had been ambushed. He would ride in and . . .

He was working this out as he rode carefully, looking around, but his mind theorizing dulled his alertness just enough so that he missed seeing the rifle barrel poking out of rocks on the trail above where he was — until it fired and then the muzzle flash caught his eye.

Instinct took over and he was already going out of the saddle and away from the bullet when it seared across his left hip. It struck the wide, thick leather of his gun belt and so it was more the impact than any penetrating damage that threw him into a spin. He seemed to corkscrew and landed heavily, and this time he didn't have the rifle!

He had pushed it back into the scabbard as holding it had become awkward when riding through a thicket that closed around himself and his mount. He had only just burst out of that thicket when the hidden gun fired.

Still rolling and skidding, Hawk managed to grasp his Remington but he saved his ammunition, squirming in behind a low rock. Gasping, short of breath from the impact of his body on the slope, he ducked as the rifle — no!

two rifles now — blasted and raked his shelter.

Then *two more* guns opened up and suddenly he was in the midst of a hornets' nest of ricocheting lead. He covered his head with his arms, another instinctive movement even if futile, and spat grit that was blasted into his mouth.

He had ridden into more than an ambush set up by a wounded man full of hate, that was for sure. There were at least four of them and they had him pinned down like a hide pegged for curing.

He had six loads in the Remington and another six in a spare cylinder in the leather pouch on his belt. It wasn't much against these odds, so he had to make every shot count. But Hawk knew he had to risk wasting at least one or two shots till he saw just how good they were.

So he thrust out the pistol's muzzle in the general direction of the bush-whackers and just as he fired, three bullets raked the rock, one driving a chip of rock against the pistol's barrel, jarring it.

OK — they were watching closely and weren't about to let him get in a position where he could take aim and maybe cause a casualty or two. But he didn't figure to just lie here and let them work around to a new position that would allow them to see into his hidey-hole so they could pick him off at their leisure.

They wouldn't figure on him making any kind of a move, simply because there wasn't anywhere for him to run. Well, there was the thicket and some rocks to his left, but both were across several yards of open ground. He gathered himself and his muscles were taut, ready to spring, when Lew Harrigan's voice called down,

'No need to die, Reb — just tell us where the rest of the gold is and we'll leave you in peace.'

'Leave me dead, more likely!' Hawk called back and Harrigan laughed.

'Oh, you been eavesdroppin'! No, Reb, where's the point? All we want is the gold. The banker told me there was 200,000 dollars' worth stole from the Healyville bank an' we got only a leetle bit of it — you and your pard Lobo know where the rest is. Tell us and we'll ride out.'

'I don't know where it is.'

'Aw, come on! Quit this stallin'. Hey, I saved your life, you know — ol' Tip here was all set to blast you good, but I talked him outta it, said we needed to talk with you first. You nailed him twice, you know. Leg wound's bleedin' all to hell but the one in his side ain't too bad, but he sure wants your scalp. You got my word I'll keep him off your neck if you tell me where the rest of the gold's buried.'

'Much obliged, Harrigan,' Hawk called sardonically. 'But reckon I'll take my chances — I really dunno where the rest of the gold is and — '

He heard the sound behind and above, a trickle of small stones or

199

coarse weathered sand caught in a crevice and disturbed now. Hawk spun onto his back, the pistol coming up, blasting two quick shots. A man up on the rockface grunted and stretched up to tiptoe as the lead slammed into him. Even as the man started to fall, Hawk saw the second one behind him, threw himself out of the way of the falling man and fired again. The second killer was bringing up his gun as the bullet drove into him and he was flung away and he scrabbled wildly for a grip, missed and toppled down to land amongst the rocks a few yards away. The first man had fallen almost beside Hawk and he was dead from the bullets. Hawk recognized him as one of the men who had helped Tip O'Malley beat him up. One of Harrigan's crew.

The other one had snapped his neck and Hawk saw he had also been there at the beating. He had no time for anything else as Harrigan swore and raked the rocks with withering fire. Both the dead men stopped wild bullets and Hawk lunged for the rocks where the man with the broken neck lay. A slug tugged at his trouser leg as he somersaulted into shelter, grabbed the dead man and pulled him on top of him between the rocks.

There was a rolling crash of rifle fire and he made himself as small as possible — but the bullets didn't seem to be hitting his shelter.

'What the . . . ?'

He sat up part way and then frowned deeply. He heard Tip O'Malley yelling something and Harrigan cursing. Then there was a smashing of brush up on the slopes, the whinnying of horses, and rapid hoof-beats.

Hawk thrust the dead man aside, grunting with the effort, gun at the ready as he worked to a crouching position. He was in time to catch a glimpse of two riders going hell for leather towards the crest of the ridge. Lew Harrigan and Tip O'Malley.

Well, who the hell had been doing all that shooting . . . ?

He soon had the answer. Two men leading horses and with smoking rifles in their hands came plodding down the slope towards him.

Hawk was startled to recognize Lobo as the one in the lead but he didn't know the second ranny, a wolf-lean type with a beard and a great hook of a nose between a couple of the meanest eyes Hawk had ever seen.

'Still gettin' yourself into trouble with the Yankees, I see,' said Lobo by way of greeting. 'You Johnny Rebs never learn, do you?'

'Didn't think I'd ever say it again, but I'm mighty glad to see you, Lobo. Who's your friend?'

'Aw, kind of a ghost I guess you'd call him. Sort of back from the dead — name's Denny Brackett.'

12

The Army

Banker Spence was never nervous when interviewing a prospective 'client' but he felt distinctly edgy and shaky when the lieutenant showed him into Captain Garrett's office.

The captain was a stiff-backed, no-nonsense career soldier and he took his job seriously. He was hard but, in the main, just. He was heading towards retirement, silver showing at his temples, brown hair thinning on top, and his trim moustache outlining his upper lip was little more than a pencil line. His eyes were direct and seemed to look right inside a man.

'Banker,' he greeted, standing and offering his hand across the desk. They shook briefly, Spence's hand limp and damp, and Garrett frowned slightly as he sat down, waved the banker to a chair, and surreptitiously wiped his hand on his uniform jacket. 'What can I do for you?'

Banker Spence licked his lips, folded his hands on top of his slim leather briefcase. He cleared his throat.

'First of all, Captain, I need to know something.'

Garrett spread his hands, indicating his willingness to listen.

'Er — if a citizen of Pagosa was — threatened, would the army be willing to provide — protection?'

Garrett frowned. 'I'm not sure what you mean, but while we're here only temporarily, certainly we would provide protection if someone was in sufficient danger to warrant it. Have you been threatened, banker?'

Spence hesitated but nodded. 'A man has threatened to harm my family and burn down my house if I don't keep silent about a certain — transaction.'

Garrett locked his fingers and leaned forward, elbows resting on his desk now. 'You intrigue me, sir. Please continue.'

Spence fidgeted with the flap of his briefcase but did not open it yet. 'Two men brought me some gold bars — Confederate gold bars. They had the usual Confederate States mint marks and the numbers check against those stolen from Healyville when the gold was on transfer from Kettledrum, just before the end of the War.'

Garrett was all ears now. 'Yes.' His tone was not very encouraging but Spence knew he couldn't stop now.

He quickly told the army captain about Harrigan and O'Malley. Then he sat back, wiping sweat from his face. 'My conscience wouldn't give me any peace — but I was afraid to speak up.'

'I can understand, I'm a family man myself. Well, this is mighty important, Banker. This is the first time any of that missing gold has turned up and — '

'Er — not quite, Captain. I had some a few months ago, just a bar or two, from Mattie North, one of the homesteaders and actually the first to prove up.'

Garrett's face hardened. 'And did she threaten you too? Is that why you didn't report it?'

Spence fidgeted. 'You weren't here then. There was trouble with Head Office and I had a lot of work to do. I used to work twenty, sometimes twenty-two hours a day until it was finished and then — well, I just didn't bother.'

'I remember hearing about your bank being in trouble — almost folded up because of some scandal with one of the directors embezzling huge amounts. It's really no excuse, Banker.'

'I know and I — I'm sorry, but — '

Garrett held up a hand. 'Leave it for now. We have something more recent to follow through on.'

Spence looked really worried. 'You'll provide my family and me with protection?'

'Yes. I'll send out an armed squad to

watch your house and family and I'll post two men outside your office at the bank.' He stood abruptly. 'I've just had an idea. This North woman is still in the infirmary, I believe. We'll hunt down Harrigan and O'Malley, who was involved in a brawl and a gunfight earlier today, but the woman might be able to tell us — *will* tell us just how she came by her gold bars. No need for you to come with me, Banker.'

Spence knew he was dismissed and he wanted nothing more than to get out of this office, but he hesitated.

'Well?' snapped Garrett and called for his orderly.

'Could I have a soldier walk me back to the bank, Captain . . . ? I'm very shaken about all this.'

He looked it, too.

Garrett sighed as the lieutenant hurried in. 'I'll arrange it. Wait outside for now. Lieutenant, I want an armed squad sent to guard this man's house and two men on duty at his bank. Arrange that and then prepare a second squad for riding. I'll lead them myself after I visit the infirmary.'

★ ★ ★

Mattie North listened to the trim captain's story and his 'request' that she tell him how she came by her gold bars.

The doctor hovered around anxiously. He had told the captain that he didn't want Mattie put through any emotional upsets at this stage and Garrett promised to be tactful. So far he had been persuasive but firm and the medic had no complaints but he refused to leave the room.

Mattie thought about the soldier's request and decided there could be little harm in telling the truth, so she gave him her story about how she had found the buried gold bars by accident, cashed one at the bank and stashed the others in the grain bin until Dunbar had stolen them.

'Harrigan and O'Malley apparently killed Dunbar for the bars they took to the bank,' she finished.

'That accounts for only five. There are still ten missing and a cashbox containing a lot of money.'

'I know nothing about that, Captain.'

'I believe you, ma'am — '

'Good of you!' Mattie said crisply.

Garrett smiled faintly. 'Yes. My problem is to find someone who can tell me where the rest of the gold is hidden — there is a substantial reward for its recovery, you know. The Union isn't so rich that it can afford to simply forget about $200,000 in gold that once belonged to an enemy . . . '

'I can't help you there.'

'Perhaps I can,' the doctor said getting their attention. 'Purdy knows something about it — he told Hawk something but I don't know the details.'

Garrett looked hard at the doctor. 'Where is this Purdy?'

'In the open infirmary section — he's badly wounded but has surprised me by recovering as much as he has. He could possibly take a brief, quiet questioning, Captain.'

Garrett started for the door. 'Let's go, Doctor.'

Mattie's teeth tugged at her lip as they left the room and then, making her decision, she pushed back the bed-clothes and slowly got out of bed.

★　★　★

Denny Brackett was a surly half-breed and regarded Hawk with suspicion. He wasn't exactly friendly towards Lobo either and Hawk figured whatever their arrangement it was one of convenience, not friendship.

'Heard you were dead, Brackett,' Hawk said as they moved away from the dead men at the ambush spot.

Brackett glared at Lobo. 'No thanks to him that I'm not. Bunch of Injuns found me and I figured what Lobo had done to me was nothin' to what they were gonna do. But there's no guessin' about Injuns. They took me back to their camp and nursed me through. Ain't many good things about bein' a half-breed but this time it paid off for me . . . they treated me good. I've been in infirmaries that never gave me better attention. Asked nothin' in return — except how to work some old Merrill muskets they'd come by. Din' ask how, but I'd heard about a wagon train that'd been attacked and a load of old rifles and out-of-date ammo bein' stolen.'

'You taught 'em how to use the guns?'

Denny Brackett snorted. ' 'Bout half of 'em — rest you couldn't use. No riflin' left, hammerlocks froze. Risky ammo and the percussion caps din' always work. But I did a little work on the best of the guns and they were happy.'

'They let you go or did you have to sneak away?'

Brackett spat to one side. 'They gimme a bag of grub and my own guns and a hoss.'

'You were lucky all right.'

'Yeah — lucky I got a chance to come after that son of a bitch there.' He jerked his head towards Lobo who smiled crookedly.

'He only wanted to find me to know if I'd found the rest of the gold.' Lobo's grin widened maddeningly.

'That was part of it,' Denny said and the look on his face told Hawk that Lobo was a dead man as far as Brackett was concerned. It was just a matter of when.

But how come they were riding together and he saved his neck? he asked. Lobo answered.

'All Denny knew was that the rest of the gang had buried their gold and the cash box somewhere in the same vicinity as the stuff Mattie found at Rockslide.' He turned to Brackett. 'You want to tell him how you found out about it?'

Brackett didn't answer right away, then he spoke matter-of-factly. 'Me and Mitch buried our gold and were ridin' out when we seen the other two, all that was left of our bunch, comin' outta the hills. We knew damn well they must've hid their part of the gold, the biggest share, 'cause we could see their saddle-bags were empty and they didn't have a pack-horse any longer. So Mitch and me bushwhacked 'em, killed Moby but only wounded Laskey.' He shook his head. 'One tough *hombre*, that Laskey. Took everythin' we handed out and just as he was dyin' said somethin' about a 'red castle'. Sounded crazy to us but we'd seen some red rock walls and wondered if that was what he meant. We looked, couldn't find nothin'. You two been workin' this range so I figured mebbe you might know this 'red castle' place. Ol' Lobo here has a notion about it, I think, but claims he can't find the way in . . . said you might know though.'

Hawk nodded, smiling crookedly. 'So you saved my bacon — ' He glanced at Lobo. 'Wondered about you getting over your threat to shoot me on sight so quickly.'

Lobo shrugged. 'My ma always said never let money come between friends.'

'Oh, we're still friends?'

'Hell, we had our diff-i-culty but I ain't one to hold a grudge.'

'Sure not if you think I might be able to find Red Canyon — and you can't.'

Lobo sobered, eyes narrowing. 'All right — I tried, but even though we seen red walls and spires of red rock I couldn't find a way in. You take us to Red Canyon, we'll do the rest.'

Hawk wondered what 'the rest' meant. They would look for the gold without his help? Or all three would try to find it and when they did . . .

Well, he figured *his* share would be paid for in lead, rather than gold.

But right now he had no choice but to show them the way to Red Canyon.

Not that it would matter all that much to these two. They would simply go to work on him until he either showed them the way or gave them directions.

Both of them seemed to be expert in making men talk after prolonged and unpleasant interrogation.

But he still had his guns.

He just hoped that when the time came he would get a chance to use them.

13

Hawks & Wolves

The doctor stopped dead in his tracks when he returned to Mattie's room.

'Good grief, woman! What d'you think you're doing?'

Mattie was standing by the end of the bed, wearing her riding clothes. She looked pale and clung to one end of the bed board for support, but he could see the determination on her face — and hear it when she spoke.

'I know enough from what Hawk has told me that the second lot of gold is supposed to be buried on my land. I'll lead Captain Garrett there.'

'You'll do nothing of the sort! You can't treat severe concussion like that! The symptoms can return for weeks to come — perhaps months.' He started towards her but something in her eyes stopped him. 'Mattie! Be reasonable. You can't really help anyone by doing this.'

'I can help Hawk. If he's out there looking for the gold, and I believe he is, he'll not only have Harrigan to contend with but Lobo, who he's had a falling-out with and now the army . . . I have to go, Doctor, I have to!'

'She's right, Doctor,' said Captain Garrett coming up. 'Purdy told me — as far as I could make out anyway — that he thinks something is buried in the back of a cave in a place called Red Canyon. He's still pretty weak, Doctor, and might need your attention.'

The doctor pushed past the soldier, muttering something about damn people coming in here and upsetting his patients, undoing all the good work he'd put in on them.

Garrett turned to Mattie.

'You really feel up to showing us the way, ma'am?'

She smiled wanly. 'I don't think I'd better comment on how I feel — but I will show you the way, Captain. I want to make sure I can point out to you a man who has helped me and shown me kindness and is only out there looking for the gold because he thinks it will help me to rebuild my place.'

'You'll be meaning this Hawk, of course. Well, as I said there is a reward. That's all anyone can expect now. Providing the gold is even found, of course.'

'I understand.'

'Here — let me take your arm. I think the sooner we ride the better.'

* * *

They kept an eye out for Harrigan and O'Malley, still not sure if there was a third man involved, but Hawk led the way almost to the country where Red Canyon was located without them seeing hide nor hair of anyone.

'They'll be up there,' Lobo said. 'Harrigan won't give up easy. O'Malley seemed to be a bit hard but he's a tough old wolf and mean as a grizzly with piles.'

'He tries to horn in, I'll blow his goddamn head off,' growled Denny Brackett and he looked at the other two. 'Or anyone else.'

'Denny, I hope you realize this is one big canyon once you get past the narrow part,' Hawk said quietly. 'It's not just a matter of going there and stepping right up to where the loot's hidden — it'll take a deal of searching.'

Brackett's eyes were flinty. 'Then we'll search. All I'm sayin' is it better not take too damn long.'

'We're not certain-sure the gold's even there, damnit!' Hawk snapped.

'It better be,' Brackett said flatly and Hawk cursed under his breath.

The man was a fool. Blinded by greed, of course, and he knew for sure that he would try to kill both Lobo and Hawk once the gold was located. Fool though he might be, he also had an innate rat-cunning, and Hawk knew that once the man saw the cave he would want to search it right away as being the most likely hiding place.

All he could do was stall a little before leading them into the actual canyon. Once inside, the fireworks would be only minutes away.

Lobo put his horse alongside Hawk as they climbed a curving trail across the face of a rise.

'I had me an idea where Red Canyon was, and it was nowheres near up this way, Hawk.'

There was a warning in his tone and Hawk glanced at him.

'But you never found it, did you?'

'No — but ain't seen any red walls up here. Quit stallin', *amigo*. I ain't got a lot of patience but Denny's got even less.'

'He's going to kill you, Lobo.'

'Know he'll try.'

'Looks like he could maybe do it — an' me as well.'

Lobo smiled crookedly. 'That beatin' must've taken more outta you than I thought.'

'The hell you two talkin' about?' Denny demanded, hauling rein and waiting for them to catch up. 'You said ride as far as this here balanced rock, Hawk. Well, we're here. Which way now? And it better not be too damn far!'

'See?' Lobo whispered. 'Told you he was losin' patience. You better produce, *amigo*, or he's gonna get real riled.'

'We turn west. On the downgrade,' Hawk said, and Denny snapped his head around, looking down the far slope.

'That'll take us back to the trail we were on an hour ago!'

'Yeah — I missed a landmark.'

'Let's not miss any more,' Brackett said flatly and jerked his head. 'You lead — straight to Red Canyon, friend.'

He was holding his rifle across his thighs and the barrel swung to point at Hawk now.

'Ride up alongside him, Lobo — an' no more talkin' or I'll cut someone's tongue out!'

Hawk couldn't push it any more. Brackett was too dangerous a man for that. He would lose patience and kill indiscriminately, worry about it afterwards — which would be way too late for Hawk and Lobo.

So Hawk led the way into Red Canyon, taking the long way round through the cutting before crossing the stream and rounding a wall that looked solid without a gap from the approach angle. He saw the surprise on Denny's face and then the man's gaze sharpened as he looked around the green grass area and up the red slope at the base of the high wall.

'By hell, if this ain't a rustler's paradise! Hey — an' is that a cave I see up there?' He glanced sharply at Lobo and then at Hawk. 'You two been holdin' out on me! *That's* where the gold'll be buried.'

'I didn't know about no cave,' Lobo protested. 'I ain't been here before.'

'Well, you're here now — and you can start diggin' when we find it.'

The rifle swung to cover them both and they stiffened. They hadn't expected Denny Brackett to tip his hand *before* the gold had been located.

'Dismount, gents, and let's get on up there. Keep your hands well away from your guns or it'll be a dead man's walk for someone.'

He let his horse walk along behind them as they moved across the canyon towards the slope leading up to the cave, rifle cocked, whistling softly between his teeth.

'Wish old Mitch was here to see this,' Brackett said and nudged his mount forward so he could kick Lobo between the shoulders. The man sprawled and had to roll quickly to get out of the way of Denny's horse's hoofs. 'But you killed him — and cut me up and left me to die! Well, you got some work to do before you go to hell, Lobo!'

He dismounted at the foot of the slope and walked on ahead to the cave mouth before gesturing for the other two to follow. It was dim inside, of course, and Brackett made them shuck their guns and toss them up against the rear wall. It was only after searching for a few minutes that he came across the mound of earth that had obviously been turned a long time ago and heaped loosely without tamping-down.

Denny kicked at it. A couple of clods came loose. 'Well, now, this looks promisin'. Hey! There's even a rusted shovel there. OK, Lobo, grab it and start diggin'. Hawk can take over when you get tired.'

Lobo said nothing, began to dig, tossing the earth behind him. Hawk frowned: it would have been easier to just dig and empty the shovel to one side. Instead, Lobo was twisting his upper body and throwing the dirt behind and up against the sloping wall.

They had to stoop where they were and Denny Brackett stood between them and the sunlit entrance, watching closely. Lobo was sweating, knee-deep in the hole by now.

'Relieve him,' Denny snapped at Hawk and the man stepped down into the hole and Lobo, with a last shovelful, twisted to throw it behind him on to the pile of dirt he had built up.

But instead of twisting all the way around, he used the movement to swing the shovel back in a blur of speed, and Denny saw it only at the last moment as the three or four pounds of dirt sailed towards him.

'Down!' shouted Lobo, thrusting Hawk aside and started to climb out of the hole.

Brackett, staggering, triggered, levered quickly and as Lobo staggered, hit, Hawk lunged out of the hole towards the place where Denny had made them throw the pistols.

A bullet ricocheted from the sloping roof and punched into the ground near him. Another made a buzzing sound as he rolled swiftly across the damp ground, snatching up one of the pistols. It was Lobo's Colt and as Denny reared up for a killing shot, Hawk thumbed the trigger three times.

Brackett twisted and spun, staggered a few steps and then went down to his knees, sobbing as he swayed. Hawk, crouching, went forward, and shot him in the back of the head.

His ears were ringing with the gunfire, and he was partially blinded by the powder flashes — which was likely why he hadn't heard Harrigan and O'Malley approaching or saw their silhouettes as they came in the cave entrance, guns in hands.

'Well, ain't you the helpful one!' Lew Harrigan laughed as he saw Denny Brackett's body and Lobo sprawled way back against the wall where Denny's shot had thrown him.

Harrigan came deeper into the cave, followed by a limping O'Malley whose eyes were blazing, not leaving Hawk.

'What's this I see?' Harrigan said, unable to keep the pleasure out of his voice. 'Why, Tip, ol' feller, I b'lieve that there's a treasure hole! Can't see any gold right now but — Hawk, drop that smokin' pistol like a good feller and get to diggin', will you? *Pronto*!'

The man's rifle jerked and Hawk let the gun fall on to the rim of the hole. O'Malley couldn't contain himself any longer and limped up quickly, swiping at Hawk with his six gun. Hawk dodged and hooked Tip on the jaw and the big man went down, weakened by loss of blood from his wounds.

Harrigan stepped in and slammed the rifle's barrel across the back of Hawk's right leg. He grunted, went down to one knee and slid into the hole. Harrigan glared down at him, kicking the shovel in on top of him.

'Dig!'

Hawk picked himself up slowly, his leg numb and unable to support his full weight. He hobbled around and started to dig, throwing the dirt out to one side, avoiding Lobo's still body. O'Malley got up slowly and Harrigan had to cuss him out when the man wanted to shoot Hawk on the spot.

They were arguing and Hawk heard the shovel blade clank against metal, looked down — and was surprised to see his own Remington Army pistol sliding into the bottom of the hole.

He didn't try to figure out how it had got there but he dropped the shovel and yelled, '*Gold*!', knowing the word would stop the others dead.

In that fraction of a second where they stared at each other and then began to swivel their gaze towards him, Hawk snatched up the Remington and, remembering he had only two loads left in the cylinder, put one into Tip O'Malley, smashing the big man down for keeps this time, then swung the gun and fired the other at Harrigan.

The rancher triggered his rifle at the same time and Hawk felt the blow in his right shoulder, the impact throwing him back into the hole, the empty gun falling from his grip.

But Harrigan was hit, too, bending in the middle, moaning as he stumbled towards the cave entrance, rifle still smoking in his hands, intent only on escape.

Hawk dragged himself out of the hole and looked for Lobo's six gun that he had dropped, couldn't find it, but crawled over Tip O'Malley's body and grabbed the man's pistol. He couldn't hold it in his right hand, fired with it in his left, heard the bullet whine off rock.

Harrigan half-turned, levering awkwardly at his rifle, still bent in the middle. His teeth bared with the effort as he brought up the weapon.

Then there was a crackle of gunfire from outside and Lew Harrigan's body arched and shuddered under the impact of lead. The rifle clattered to the ground and he crumpled, dead before he sprawled on the floor of the cave.

Ears ringing wildly, gritting his teeth against the pain of his shoulder wound, Hawk knelt there, the pistol sagging in his left hand. He watched, bewildered, as half a dozen soldiers swarmed in, a man he later saw was a lieutenant pointing a pistol at him and yelling at him to let his gun drop.

Hawk did so and then they were surrounding him and he thought to turn his head and look at Lobo. The man was right on the back edge of the hole now, one arm dangling over the broken earth, staring at Hawk, face gaunt and grey.

Ignoring the lieutenant's order to stay put, Hawk crawled across to Lobo.

'You hit bad?'

'Couple busted ribs, I reckon.'

'Thanks for pushing my gun into the hole.'

'I kinda owed you — somethin'. Wasn't ready for Denny cuttin' loose.'

'You did OK — hell, we both did OK!'

Then the cave was full of people, soldiers milling around, Captain Garrett calling up his medical orderly to treat Hawk's and Lobo's wounds.

And Mattie North, looking pale and tired, coming in to kneel beside him as the medic knotted off the sling for Hawk's right arm.

'I led the army in here — I was afraid we might be too late.'

'Glad to see you any time — but you look beat. You ought to be resting in bed.'

'Oh, not you, too! I've put up with the doctor admonishing me and the captain fussing every foot of the way up here from Pagosa — I'm beginning to feel like a sick old woman.'

Hawk managed a grin, but his shoulder was really hurting now. 'You still look good to me.'

Even in the dim light of the cave he saw her blush — and the pleasure that came to her face at the same time.

Garrett had set two men to digging in the hole and one of the soldiers called, 'Eight bars here, Cap'n — and that's it.'

'Well, better than I expected. No sign of a metal cash box?'

'No, sir, and as you can see, we've widened the hole to hell an' gone — '

'Watch your mouth, soldier! There's a lady present!'

'Sorry, sir — sorry, ma'am.'

Garrett gave his orders and the lieutenant supervised the loading of gold into leather panniers they had brought. Garrett came and stood over Hawk and Lobo, who was being strapped up in tight bandages by the medic and his helper.

'Well, you two are still on the books as deserters,' he said grimfaced. He let them think about that and Mattie said,

'But the War's long finished, Captain. Surely their crime isn't still answerable.'

'Ma'am, the Army never forgets, can't afford to. But let me see . . . Lobo and Hawk.' He studied some papers he was holding. 'Mmmm — they answer the descriptions all right but looks like I've got the names wrong . . . Myron Hatfield and Christian Winters. Well, I suppose Lobo and Hawk could be nicknames. You, Lobo — your name Winters?'

'No, sir, Cap'n.'

'And Hawk — your name Hatfield?'

'No, Cap'n.'

'You'd both swear that's the truth? In

the name of the Holy Bible?'

'Yessir!' they said together and he nodded.

'Well, that's good enough for me — I suppose as you actually found the missing gold you'll be entitled to the reward. Not the full amount because there're still two bars missing and the cash, but it should be a tidy sum.'

Hawk looked at Mattie. 'Reckon you'll be able to rebuild now and prove up on the whole section.'

'But that money's yours, Hawk.'

'You've taken on too much. You need a partner to get all that land developed properly.'

She smiled. 'Well, I hadn't really thought of taking on a partner, but — it does have some appeal.'

There was a twinkle in her eye as she said that.

* * *

Three weeks later, Lobo announced that he thought it was time to push on.

233

He was pretty well recovered from his wound and his ribs were knitting, though still in a brace of firm bandages.

'You're going before you collect the reward?' Hawk asked him.

Lobo shrugged. 'You keep it for me — put it to use rebuildin' the spread for Mattie. I'll come back sometime and collect.'

Hawk frowned and Mattie threw her arms about Lobo and held him tightly. 'Don't go, Lobo. We need you to help finish the house.'

'I'm no carpenter, Mattie. No, it's time for me to move on. I've got used to not standin' still in the one place these past few years. Hawk's a good man. You'll have a fine spread here eventually.'

They couldn't talk him out of it and he rode out just before sundown and they watched him out of sight from the stoop of the new cabin that was only partially completed.

'Will he come back like he said?' Mattie asked.

'I'm not sure,' Hawk said slowly and thoughtfully. 'I don't really know Lobo all that well when you get right down to it.'

She wondered what he meant but he didn't explain.

★   ★   ★

Hawk rode out before sunup the next morning, careful not to wake the girl who was sleeping in the room he had finished off for her.

Once he had cleared the ranchyard he spurred the black into the hills.

He rode into Red Canyon at mid-morning, the sun blazing down from the walls and filling the place with a crimson light. He dismounted, led his horse in over the stream and through the hidden gap in the wall.

At the bottom of the slope where the cave was, he saw Lobo's mount, hobbled and grazing on a patch of grass.

Hawk smiled thinly: *he had been right*.

He hurried across, climbed the slope slowly, still getting a twinge from his shoulder wound, and heard the clang of metal coming from inside the cave. He eased through the entrance so that he wasn't silhouetted and saw Lobo had his back to him, smashing at a lock on a dirt-spattered metal box about two feet by one by eighteen inches deep.

Hawk knew it was the missing cash box from the robbery, and he also knew why Lobo had been throwing the dirt he had dug behind him instead of to one side. He had used the shovelfuls of dirt to cover a second mound of earth before Denny Brackett could see it.

Purdy had told Hawk there were small mounds at the rear of the cave. The cash box had been buried separately to the gold bars — why he didn't know, but then who could know the way a couple of renegade bank robbers would think? Perhaps the gold was one man's share, the box of cash the second man's.

Suddenly the hinges squeaked as

Lobo lifted the lid and he thrust his hands in, brought them out holding neatly stacked sheaves of bills. He still hadn't seen Hawk. Lobo sat back on his hams, chuckling — and then suddenly the chuckling stopped and Lobo held the packages of money closer to his face, turning it towards the light.

That was when he saw Hawk and he dropped the money and his hand whipped back to his gun butt.

Hawk held out his left hand. 'Easy, Lobo — I was just curious. Figured you'd left the cashbox for yourself.'

Lobo stared hard and then lowered the Colt. 'Figured it'd be easier to handle than gold, seein' as the banks still have to report on any gold bars that come their way.'

'Looks to be a lot there — more than the gold's worth.'

'Yeah — hundred thousand easy. Mebbe more.'

Hawk whistled. 'Hell almighty, man! That's real *dinero*.'

'That's where you're wrong, Hawk,

237

old pard. It *ain't* real. It's Confederate scrip. Be good for startin' a campfire or paperin' a wall to keep out the draughts, but even the whole cashbox-full wouldn't buy you a cup of coffee.'

Hawk stared, felt his mouth sagging. 'Well, I'll be . . . two hundred thousand bucks, some in gold, mostly in cash. Only the Confederacy lost the War and the cash is worthless.' He paused and his mouth twitched. 'Kind of funny, eh?'

'Funny? By God, you got a queer sense of humour! I been dreamin' of this for years and now — ' He stopped, face tight and suddenly it began to loosen up. 'Well — it is some joke, ain't it! Damn expensive but still a goddamn *joke*!'

They had a brief laugh about it, examined the bills to make sure they were worthless and then Lobo put them back into the hole.

He began to shovel in the dirt on top of the box. 'Let someone else find it one day and see how they feel.'

'What you gonna do now, Lobo? There's still your share of the reward.'

'Told Mattie she could use that.'

'All right — then that'll give you a third share in the spread.'

Lobo stopped shovelling, leaned on the handle. 'Me? A rancher . . . ?'

'Not so bad, is it?'

'I — dunno.'

'Well, you could do worse. We still pards or not?'

Hawk held out his hand and Lobo frowned down at it, looked into Hawk's face and dropped the shovel, gripping firmly, causing Hawk to wince at the pain that shot up into his shoulder.

But he didn't mind.

They were still Lobo and Hawk — pardners.

THE END

We do hope that you have enjoyed reading this large print book.

Did you know that all of our titles are available for purchase?

We publish a wide range of high quality large print books including:
Romances, Mysteries, Classics
General Fiction
Non Fiction and Westerns

Special interest titles available in large print are:
The Little Oxford Dictionary
Music Book, Song Book
Hymn Book, Service Book

Also available from us courtesy of Oxford University Press:
Young Readers' Dictionary
(large print edition)
Young Readers' Thesaurus
(large print edition)

For further information or a free brochure, please contact us at:
Ulverscroft Large Print Books Ltd.,
The Green, Bradgate Road, Anstey,
Leicester, LE7 7FU, England.
Tel: (00 44) **0116 236 4325**
Fax: (00 44) **0116 234 0205**

Soon the paddle steamer would be on its long journey down the Missouri River to St Louis. Now, all Saul Rhymer had to do was to play the last master stroke of the evening. He looked at the mounting pile of gold and dollar bills and again at the cards in his hand. Then, looking around the table, he produced the deed to the goldmine in Montana. 'Let's play poker!' But little did he know how that journey back to St Louis would change his life so drastically.

THE ARIZONA KID

Andrew McBride

When former hired gun Calvin Taylor took the job of sheriff of Oxford County, New Mexico, it was for one reason only — to catch, or kill, the notorious Arizona Kid, and pick up the fifteen hundred dollars reward the governor had secretly offered. Taylor found himself on the trail of the infamous gang known as the Regulators, hunting down a man who'd once been his friend. The pursuit became, in every sense, a journey of death.